Amazing Hunting Survival Stories

Wilderness Adventure Tales that Teach Practical Skills & Inspire Extraordinary Perseverance

Phoenix MacLeod

Legal Notice

This book is copyright-protected and only for personal use. You cannot reproduce, duplicate, amend, distribute, transmit, sell, use, quote, or paraphrase any part or portion of the content without the author's or publisher's direct written consent and permission.

Under no circumstances will any blame or legal responsibility be held against the publisher or author for any damages, reparation, or monetary loss due to the information contained within this book. Either directly or indirectly. You are responsible for your own choices, actions, and results.

Disclaimer

Please note that the information in this document is for educational and entertainment purposes only. This book's content has been derived from various sources. All effort has been expended to present accurate, up-to-date, reliable, and complete information. No warranties of any kind are declared or implied.

Readers acknowledge that the author and publisher are not engaging in rendering medical, legal, financial, or professional advice. He is not a medical doctor or a physician. Please consult a licensed medical professional with concerns about your health or specific medical conditions before attempting any methods or techniques this book outlines.

By reading this document, the reader agrees that the author or publisher is under no circumstances responsible for any direct or indirect losses incurred from using the information contained within this document, including, but not limited to, errors, omissions, or inaccuracies.

Contents

Introduction

It's in the heart of the wild, where each rustling of the leaves sings its own song and each footprint on the ground leaves its own mark, that we find a realm of incredible tales of human survival against impossible odds.

In all its undeniable beauty, the wilderness is nothing to be taken lightly. If you're like most people, you're used to the comforts of having a bed to sleep in at home, food and water you can take out of the refrigerator at any time, and a shower so you can stay clean.

While you may admire the majesty of the wild based on what you've seen in photographs or experienced on camping or hiking trips, have you ever thought about what you would do to survive if you found yourself stranded in the middle of nowhere?

What if you sustained an ankle injury on a hiking trip that prevented you from walking out? What if your kayak capsized in a river and left you stranded along a riverbank? What if a blizzard suddenly set in while you were hunting for deer on a mountainside?

Suddenly, the wilderness doesn't seem so serene after all.

My own story of survival didn't start near the Appalachian Mountains of Kentucky, where I grew up. Instead, it started across the world in the South Pacific. When we were younger, my wife and I were called to serve as missionaries to people in a remote jungle village in Papua New Guinea.

We invested seven years of our lives in that ministry, sleeping under mosquito nets in our solar-powered hut and learning how the nationals lived off the land, swamps, and river in the thick rainforest.

In photographs I had seen, the jungle was always lush, green, and vibrant. It was beautiful. Once we began living in it, however, all the beauty was accompanied by the unpleasant reality of nonstop malaria-bearing mosquitoes latching onto our skin, thick humidity bringing mildew to all leather, and incessant rains flooding our village.

While, thankfully, we were never stranded in the jungle, we were exposed every day to what wilderness survival required. Together, we battled malaria and other tropical diseases, learned bushcraft skills to build shelters out of entirely natural resources, collected and purified water, found ways to store our food safely, built fires while it was pouring rain, and applied first aid skills with little to no medical resources for ourselves or the villagers.

It was a very trying time, both physically and mentally, but even though it tested my resolve, it also deepened my character. It enabled me to build my survival skills in ways I never could have otherwise. I'm very grateful for my years in the South Pacific, and it was those experiences that offered me real-world insight into what living off-grid in the wild is truly like. When my wife and I returned home to Kentucky to raise our family, we were well-prepared to live off the land in our rural homestead.

During our time living in the jungle of Papua New Guinea and the years since while hunting the mountains and valleys of Kentucky, I couldn't help but wonder: What if I get lost and stranded out here?

BUT IT'S NOT MY story I want to share throughout this book. Instead, I want to share nine realistic tales of characters who found themselves stranded in the wilderness. This book provides heroic stories of young hunters who found themselves in harrowing life-or-death situations and were forced to rely on courage, resilience, and resourcefulness to survive.

Each of the hunters in these stories survived because of two primary perspectives: their mindset and their respect for the wild. The wilderness will test your physical and mental limits to the maximum, but it also provides all of the resources you need to make it out. While living in Papua New Guinea, I learned firsthand that we need to learn how to access and use these resources by working in harmony with nature rather than against it.

It's precisely the people who work against nature who tragically rarely make it out. But the people who work with it and have the unwavering determination to make it out are those who return to their loved ones.

Each of the nine chapters herein will consist of a heroic survival story followed by an overview of the survival skills utilized by the characters in the story. Consider each chapter as a stepping stone toward becoming a master of the wilderness, learning essential skills that might one day be priceless to you.

So, fellow explorers, embark with me on this journey of survival and discover the untold tales that weave together time-tested knowledge and the indomitable human spirit. The wild awaits—are you ready to unlock its secrets?

If so, turn the page. As you'll soon see, survival is not just a skill; it's an art.

Then you can gain additional **Survival Wisdom from an Off-Grid Survivor** at www.PhoenixMacleod.com

I

Canoeing in the Cascades

Cascade Mountains, Oregon

The dawn painted the sky in hues of pink and gold over the flowing waters of a river located deep in the Cascade Mountains. The air carried the crisp scent of pine, and the distant morning calls of birds echoed through the towering trees that stood as monuments to nature.

With each stroke of the paddle, Will Cameron's canoe glided forward gracefully, leaving ripples in its wake. The forest embraced him on both sides of the river.

Will's eyes were keen, and his senses were heightened. He propelled forward with his paddle strokes and his determination.

It was October 10th, a date Will looked forward to every year. It was the date his father had taken him on this annual mule deer hunting trip. They would load up their canoe and paddle it up to the hunting grounds nestled far in the interior of the mountains.

The grounds would take several days to reach on foot but could be accessed by canoe within hours. No one else knew about the grounds, and Will's father and father before him would bag a buck there yearly.

This was Will's second year going on the trip alone. When cancer had tragically taken his father two years ago, Will was intimidated at the thought of venturing up in the canoe by himself as a 23-year-old just out of college. His young wife, Charlotte, tried to talk him out of it. But Will was determined to do just as he and his father had done for years.

He knew that traditions were important and that he needed to put venison on the table for his family. He also knew that one day, he and his young son Hunter would venture out like his father had taken him out before. He needed a few years of solo experience on this trip to be ready to teach his son when the time came.

CLAD IN EARTH-TONED CLOTHING, Will blended seamlessly with the natural colors of the wilderness. A wide-brimmed hat shielded his eyes from the early morning sun, revealing a young face that was weathered by the countless trips into the mountains. His small hunting pack was stowed in the front of his canoe and carried his essentials: water, satellite phone, energy bars, freeze-dried food pack, a compact first aid kit, blanket, poncho, extra pair of socks, matches, and an area map for navigating.

His rifle, a venerable Swedish-made Husqvarna Mauser-style .308 Winchester with a walnut stock his father had given him, was wrapped in a towel and resting against his pack. His knife was strapped in its leather sheath to his hip. He did not carry a pistol. Will always preferred to travel as lightly as possible and forgo carrying anything he did not consider necessary.

His canoe, crafted from lightweight yet durable materials, had a sleek design allowing nimble maneuvering around the rocks that jutted out of the water. This was a crucial feature when navigating the unpredictable currents of the Cascade's rivers, which Will was accustomed to.

As he negotiated the river bends with skillful strokes of the paddle, Will closed his eyes to embrace the serenity of the river. There were no rapids ahead that he would need to worry about, so he remained confident in keeping his eyes closed and put himself into an almost meditative state while his arms paddled forward, almost on instinct.

Suddenly, Will lurched forward as the canoe came to an abrupt halt. The canoe had struck a hidden obstacle with a sudden and jarring force. The impact caught Will off guard, and the vessel tipped sideways. Immediately, his serene meditation was shattered as he plunged violently into the cold river.

BAM!

Will's head collided directly with a rock that was under the water. The force of the blow dazed him, but he managed to return to the surface.

The water, once his calming companion, had become a turbulent adversary. Will fought against the current, struggling to maintain the surface and catch his breath while dazed from the collision with the rock. Gasping for air and with his vision blurred, he frantically looked around and searched for the canoe. He could make out that it was turned over and being carried away by the river's relentless flow.

A shockwave of pain went through Will's skull as he floated downriver. As the jarring pain set in, his head and neck movements started to slow. He thrashed his arms about, trying to grab onto something – anything. It felt like an eternity before he finally managed to clutch onto a nearby rock to steady himself.

Will pulled himself forward to the jutting rock and aimed towards the riverbank. He placed his feet against the rock, then pushed forward to propel himself to the bank. The river's current carried Will into the shallows, and he dragged against the pebbles and dirt underneath the water.

Burying his fingers into the dirt, Will managed to claw himself onto the riverbank until he was partly out of the water. Blood trickled from a gash on his forehead, coloring the water and dirt around him.

His head throbbing, Will closed his eyes, almost as if to put himself into the meditative state he'd been in before.

Moments later, he passed out.

IN THE CAMERONS' TRANQUIL Oregon suburb home, the morning sunlight filtered through the curtains, casting a warm, yellowish glow on

Charlotte's anxious face. With each passing minute, her anxiety deepened, and the silence that lingered in the absence of Will's usual call had become unbearable.

Their routine was supposed to be the same as last year's. Once he reached the hunting grounds in the late morning, he would call her with his satellite phone to let her know he was safe. Then, that night, he would call her again to let her know how he was doing. He would stay out for a maximum of two nights and come back the following morning, regardless of whether he had brought down a mule deer or not.

But he still hadn't called.

Charlotte's mind raced with a torrent of thoughts, each moment without news of Will amplifying the knot twisting in her stomach.

Hunter played with his toys, but Charlotte could tell he was starting to grow uneasy, too.

Attempting to maintain normalcy as best she could, Charlotte scooped Hunter up in her arms and held him close. His questioning gaze met hers, as if he were making a silent plea for reassurance that she couldn't provide.

"Daddy just went on a little adventure, sweetheart," Charlotte whispered, her voice laced with a forced calmness that barely concealed the anxiety beneath the surface. "But he'll be back soon. Mommy just needs to check on him."

As she slowly guided Hunter back to his toys on the floor, her eyes became fixed on the clock above the mantelpiece and the seconds ticked away like a drumbeat.

WILL SLOWLY OPENED HIS eyes as he regained consciousness on the riverbank.

Only halfway out of the river, his clothes were soaked to the skin and covered in dirt and sand.

Dazed and disoriented, the world around Will swirled in a hazy blur as he grappled with the realization that something had gone wrong. Slowly, he began to remember being thrown from the canoe and hitting his head on the rock.

Pain radiated from the back of his head like a furnace, and as he tentatively touched his forehead, Will's fingers came away stained with blood. Upon seeing the red on his fingers, his instincts kicked in.

He struggled to his feet, the ground unsteady beneath him like an earthquake. The river's current had washed him ashore, leaving him battered and bruised, but the head injury was making it difficult for him to coordinate his movements. He staggered forward and fell to his knees. Steadying himself on his hands, he managed to pick himself up again and stand.

As he took stock of his surroundings, Will realized the urgency of tending to his head injury first and foremost and then getting warm and dry. The dampness clung to his clothes, and in a matter of hours, the chilling evening air would exacerbate the effects of the cold water on his body.

On instinct, Will reached for the blue bandana he kept in his pocket. He hastily wrapped it around his head to stem the bleeding from the gash on his forehead. The makeshift bandage provided a temporary solution, but Will knew he needed to find shelter and warmth quickly.

WILL FELT AROUND HIS body. His fixed-blade knife was still strapped to his side in its sheath, and he had the small box of matches in his pocket that he always kept there when he went hunting or hiking in the woods. Those matches would become his lifeline. His fingers fumbled as he retrieved the small box, and with a mixture of relief and determination, he contemplated the dry wood and foliage not far from the riverbank.

Despite the throbbing pain in his head, Will stumbled towards the wood growth in front of him. It dawned on him that his survival pack and beloved hunting rifle had been lost in the capsized canoe, but he was in no mood to let that bother him now. He would set aside his anger and frustration until later.

Will gathered leaves, twigs, and branches into a small kindling pile by the riverbank. He knew it was important to be more strategic about choosing a campsite, but he was in a rush. He could build a fire here and now and then move it somewhere else if needed.

Will reached into his matchbox with shaking fingers. Several matches flooded out of the box and onto the dirt below him until he finally managed to get one pinched between his finger and thumb.

He struck the match twice against the box until it generated a small flame, then held it to the outside of the tinder pile.

It went out.

Will tried to pick up more matches from the ones that had fallen to the ground. He finally managed to pinch one and strike it against the box. This time, he placed the new flame into the center of the kindling pile and released the match.

He bent over to blow into the flames from the side of the pile. The flame grew slowly and took over more of the kindling in a fiery dance. Gradually, Will picked up more small sticks and dried leaves he could find around him and placed them into the growing fire.

The sound of the crackling flames seemed to offer a reprieve from the cold, but Will knew it was purely a mental relief rather than an actual, physical one. He needed to get warm and dry fast, or else hypothermia would set in once the sun disappeared behind the mountains.

He gathered more wood, picking up sticks and fallen branches from the ground and throwing some of them into the fire and others into a pile as spare firewood for the night. When satisfied with the pile he had built, Will allowed himself to collapse next to the fire.

He untied his boots, removed them, and set them next to the fire to dry before removing his wet clothes. Then he sat up against a tree, exhausted, and stared into the orange flames.

As the fire flickered and danced, casting a glow on the riverbank, Will's thoughts turned back to the loss of his rifle and supplies from the capsized canoe. The sadness over the loss of his father's rifle morphed into a realization of the gravity of the situation—he was alone, injured, and far from civilization.

Yet Will was an experienced hunter. Even though he had never found himself in a predicament this serious before, he was equipped with the essential knowledge he had gleaned from all his time in the wild. Will mentally prepared himself for the challenges ahead, determined to build what shelter he could before darkness fell and then navigate the wilderness in the morning to find his way back home.

THE MORNING HAD COME and gone, and the quietness left by the absence of Will's scheduled call grew more pronounced. By the time the sun set that evening, Charlotte's worry had solidified into a resolve to take action.

She picked up her smartphone, her fingers briefly hesitating over the keypad before dialing emergency services. When the phone rang, the calm voice on the other end asked what she needed, and Charlotte recounted the details of Will's canoeing expedition and his failure to contact her as scheduled.

"He was supposed to have called me by ten, eleven at the latest," Charlotte spoke, her voice wavering. "It's seven now, and I still haven't heard from him. What can you do to find him?"

The dispatcher's assurance that they would send an emergency rescue team to Will's most recently known location provided some comfort. Still, Charlotte knew she couldn't sleep over her fear and worry about what could be happening to Will.

As the night deepened, Will sat as close as he could to the crackling fire on the riverbank. His makeshift shelter, little more than a lean-to, had become a refuge against the biting chill. The flames' glow cast shadows on the trees surrounding him.

The cold had seeped into his bones, and he knew maintaining his body heat was paramount. Having stripped down to his undergarments, he had wrung out the excess water from his clothes and set them near the fire. And the warmth from the flames gradually began to chase away his chill.

Realizing the need for a more substantial shelter, Will surveyed the area for materials. Moving back and forth between the woods (to collect some materials) and the fire (for warmth), he methodically gathered branches and foliage. Positioning a longer pole horizontally between two trees, he laid several more sticks against the pole in the direction the wind was coming from. He then layered the boughs of trees over those sticks for insulation. The makeshift structure, though rudimentary, offered a simple barrier against the wind, a crucial step in ensuring Will's survival through the night.

As he waited for his clothes to dry, with his back to the lean-to wall, Will contemplated his next steps. The loss of his rifle and supplies was a stark reality that he couldn't change, and he needed to formulate a plan to navigate the wilderness and, if possible, signal for help.

As the night wore on, Will monitored the fire, fueling it with the gathered wood to keep the flames alive. The river's gentle murmur provided a cool backdrop, almost as a lullaby for Will to fall asleep.

Will went to sleep over a bed of boughs he had assembled on the ground as he planned his morning. He would follow the river downstream, a decision motivated by the increased likelihood of encountering signs of civilization near a source of water. His father had always reminded him of this fact when they went hunting together.

Before setting out, Will also decided he would fashion a fire bundle (a package of kindling that he could wrap with birch bark) and carry it with him as he went. The bundle would act as both a makeshift signaling device by the smoke it created and a faster means of getting a larger fire going if and when he needed to.

WHEN HE AWOKE TO the dawn of a new morning, Will didn't waste time before he rolled up. The fire was still going, a testament to his discipline of getting up every two hours to throw more wood on it. That was another practice Will had learned from his father. Starting when Will was twelve, his father always made him trade nights for who had "fire watch."

Will found that his clothes were still somewhat damp, yet much dryer and warmer than the preceding evening, especially the inside of his boots. It was vital that his boots be as dry as possible to prevent any possibility of developing trench foot during his walkout. With his head still throbbing, he gingerly dressed for the big day ahead.

He soaked the bandana in the river and pressed it against his forehead. The bandana had succeeded in stopping the bleeding from the open cut on his head, but he would still have to keep the wound covered at all times to reduce the risk of infection.

Will also knew that his highest priority (in addition to finding a way out) was to get hydrated. He had a limitless source of running water available to him but no cup or means to store the water or even a way to know if it was safe to drink in the first place. But he needed water now. Without any medicine, hydration would be the only relief he could have from his pounding headache.

To craft a water filter from natural materials, Will first used his knife to cut away some bark from a birch tree and rolled the bark into a cone. He cut some thread from one of his shoelaces to wrap around the bottom of the filter to hold it together.

Will then began using his other gathered materials to create the filter media. First, he layered the internal bottom of the bark cone with leaves and small pebbles, creating a barrier to prevent the smaller elements from passing through the opening at the bottom. On top of the pebbles, he added a layer of fine sand collected from the riverbank, which would act as the primary filtration component, designed to capture smaller particles and invisible impurities. Finally, he placed another broad leaf with holes punctured using the knife on the uppermost layer to hold the filtering materials in place.

Kneeling by the river's edge, Will carefully directed water into the top of his makeshift filter. While soaking the bandana in the river with one hand, he positioned his mouth under the opening of the filter, which he held in the other. He repeatedly fed water from the bandana by squeezing it out and re-soaking it until clean water slowly flowed out from the bark cone base into Will's dry mouth.

He continued this routine for twenty minutes, taking in as much water as possible. Then he soaked the bandana in the river again and wrapped it around his forehead again to act as a cool compress against the cut.

Re-energized by the water, Will walked next to the river downstream with his fire bundle in one hand and a pole serving as a walking stick to help balance himself. The fire bundle had been wrapped tightly with a shoelace and birch bark, much like the filter.

Will filled the bundle with green leaves and pieces of brush and added smoldering kindling to the top, which he continued to blow into to keep burning. Slowly, the green vegetation held within the birch bark wrapping began to smolder and generate white smoke that Will hoped would rise to pierce the tree line to alert potential rescuers.

The throbbing in Will's head was still there. Each time he felt dizzy, he permitted himself time to sit down and rest next to the river. He knew he hadn't called Charlotte for over a full day and that she had promised to send out rescuers in that event. He felt comforted knowing there were people out looking for him and he could also rely on the river to lead him to people eventually.

THE SEARCH TEAM, EQUIPPED with advanced tracking technology and knowledge of the terrain, combed through the wilderness from a helicopter above. Their efforts intensified as they approached the general location provided during Charlotte's emergency call, the same spot where Will had launched his canoe into the river. The sun hung low in the sky, casting long shadows on the forest floor.

As the rescue team navigated the terrain from above, one member noticed a subtle movement along the riverbank. Something caught another's eye—a glimpse of a trail of smoke rising above the trees, as if waving its arms in a desperate plea for attention. Their hearts quickened with the realization that they had likely located their target.

The rescuers followed the smoke to an opening by the river. Their eyes fixed on a distant silhouette waving his arms and appearing to call out.

The rescue team, clad in orange and equipped with medical supplies, lowered a man onto the ground. He confirmed it was Will, whose ordeal was now over the morning after it had all begun.

He was transported to Peacehealth Medical Center to be assessed and treated. He was soon cleared to return home and advised to rest and heal from his concussion.

THE BEST THING WILL had done on the day he departed for his excursion was to ask Charlotte to find help if he didn't call her as scheduled. Had Will not done this, it's a certainty he would have spent more time trying to walk his way out. He had also done well to get a fire going as soon as possible to dry out his clothes, and by packing the fire with him in the wrapped birch bark, he could generate smoke for signaling as he walked.

Besides the fire, the birch bark itself had been perhaps Will's greatest ally during the entire ordeal, being used to wrap both his makeshift water filter and his fire bundle. The white smoke from the bundle alerted the rescuers to his presence and then directed them to his precise location.

When Charlotte and Hunter appeared in the lobby upon his release, they embraced him tightly.

2

Frozen Whiteout

Rocky Mountains, Idaho

The Rocky Mountains stretched out in all directions before James Munro and his 14-year-old daughter Avery. High up on the mountainside, the aroma of pine permeated the air and intermingled with the crisp scent of freshly fallen snow.

The mountainside they had ascended had become a rolling terrain of rises and falls dotted with evergreen pine trees. Though their boughs were laden and drooped with heavy coats of snow, the trees stood tall and proud, with their crests reaching upwards as if trying to touch the gray sky.

The rocky outcrops, coated in more layers of white, added a rugged texture to the landscape. An icy chill accompanied a howl in the air. James and Avery were indeed in a remote corner of the world.

The ground beneath their boots was a carpet of white snow, untouched except for their bootprints and the occasional series of hooved prints left from deer or elk that had been here before them. The latter was their quarry.

THIS WAS THE FIRST of James's annual elk trips, on which he had brought Avery along. She had always begged him to let her join one of his 'real hunting trips,' not just a quick squirrel or grouse hunt like he would take her along on fall afternoons after school. Last year was supposed to be the year that Avery could join once she became a teenager, but a sprained calf from running track had prevented that. So this year ended up being her first instead.

James was a solitary hunter and a strong man. Usually, against the advice of most of his other hunting buddies, he would hunt these mountainsides alone. When he harvested an elk, he would quarter the animal before hiking back down to his truck with one quarter over his shoulders and then repeating the trek three additional times. It was hardly efficient, but James always enjoyed walking up and down a mountainside. In his perspective, exercising in nature certainly beats running on the treadmill at the gym.

Both James and Avery were warmly dressed. They had to be to block the frosty air and chilly winds. James wore a weather-resistant jacket over a fleece-lined thermal shirt, insulated waterproof pants, and sturdy boots. He had a compact yet heavy pack loaded with supplies strapped to his back, and his scoped Sako Model 85 .300 Win Mag rifle was slung over his shoulder.

Following her father's lead, Avery wore a thick parka with a fur-lined hood, a cozy knit sweater underneath (which her mother Bonnie had made), insulated snow pants, another layer of sweat pants underneath, and winter boots. Both wore snug-fitting orange beanies over their heads to keep their ears covered.

JAMES HAD ALWAYS WARNED Avery that it could get frigid up in these mountains. She was annoyed when he and her mother had her wear multiple layers of warm clothes, believing it was excessive.

But now that she was on the mountain with her father, Avery wondered if she had dressed warmly enough. She tried to hide her shivering, but to no avail.

"Remember what I said about these mountains, Avery," James said. "The weather can be unpredictable up here."

"Yeah, yeah, I remember," said Avery. "But it's not *that* cold."

Her father managed a wry chuckle. "You're tougher than you think, kiddo, but the mountains always have their own way of reminding us who's in charge."

"What are you saying?" she asked.

James gestured to the gathering clouds overhead. "Look up there. Looks like we might be in for more than just a bit of cold."

Avery squinted at the sky, the annoyance from her thoughts about the clothes momentarily forgotten. What little sunlight had managed to filter through the thick canopy of gray clouds above was being pulled back into the sky, casting a dim shadow over the landscape. The clouds seemed to darken as well. It was already starting to snow a little.

"You think it's going to start snowing harder?" Avery asked.

James nodded. "Or worse. We may have to cut this one short."

Avery felt a rock form and then sink to her stomach at the thought that they would go home empty-handed. James noticed her apprehension.

"It's okay," he said as he put an arm around her shoulder. "You don't get one every time you come out."

The wind picked up, and the snow fell a little harder.

"We need to get off this mountain," he continued. "We're too exposed out here in the open."

THEY STARTED TO WORK their way back the same way they had come. As they walked along, the wind increased, carrying a biting chill that cut through their layers like a knife through paper. The falling snowflakes danced in a frenzy around them.

"Over there." James gestured to a pine tree where they could find temporary relief from the growing snowfall. Looking at his daughter, James could tell she was very cold. "We may have to make shelter. I don't see this letting up anytime soon."

"Shelter?" Avery asked. "What's wrong with just heading back down to the truck?"

James shook his head. "Going downhill in a snowstorm is riskier."

"Why?" she asked.

James tried to peer through the falling snowfall, but visibility rapidly decreased.

"We won't be able to see where we're going," he replied. "It's not smart to walk downhill over uneven terrain where we can't even see the obstacles. We'll find a good spot to build a shelter and wait it out. Come on."

Avery nodded, a newfound appreciation for her father's caution settling in.

James led them to a group of pine trees for protection as the snowstorm bore down on them. It was clear the snow wasn't stopping. As she had that morning, Avery couldn't even see the other mountain peaks anymore.

The dense evergreen canopy provided somewhat of a natural barrier against the wind and swirling snow, but it wouldn't be enough. They were still cold and would drop further once night hit.

James surveyed the surroundings and selected a spot where the trees stood closely together.

"There," he said.

"What are we doing?" Avery asked.

"Building a snow trench," James responded.

He knelt by the trees and picked up a stick to outline the rectangular boundaries of the snow trench.

"Dig," James instructed.

Wearing their insulated gloves, he and Avery began to remove the snow from the outline he had made.

"Are we going to camp here?!" Avery asked, her voice wavering a bit.

"Only for as long as we need to," James reported.

As Avery continued to dig into the snow, James placed the excavated snow around the outline's perimeter, forming an additional barrier against the wind.

The trench began to take shape, its walls gradually rising as they carved deeper into the snowpack. Once the trench was about three feet deep, six feet long, and two feet wide, James indicated for them to stop.

"Okay, okay," James said. "How are you doing?"

"Fine," Avery said, but she was still shivering beneath her layered clothes; she knew her dad didn't believe her.

The snow was still falling hard, and even with the trees above them blocking some of it, it wouldn't take long for their trench to refill.

"Okay, start gathering as many sticks and boughs as you can," James instructed with authority. "Use your knife to cut the boughs from the trees."

As Avery collected the boughs and sticks, James arranged the sticks horizontally over the top of the trench to serve as the roof. He placed the sticks close to one another to keep the open spaces minimal. Then he layered the pine boughs over the sticks, placing them close together.

When the snow trench was completed with its stick-and-bough roof, it served as a cozy nook nestled within the wintry landscape. James ran out from the shelter of the collection of pine trees to the rocky outcrops, picking up rocks and carrying them back to place on the end of the boughs to anchor them down.

"Get inside," James said.

James and Avery huddled inside their snow trench. They placed their packs at the opening to serve as a makeshift door, with the compartments facing inward. James laid his rifle over his torso.

As they lay there side-by-side, their breath visible in the chilly air, James gave Avery a reassuring glance.

"We'll wait out the storm here," he said, his voice a steady anchor amid the swirling chaos.

Outside, the winds howled and all that could be seen was a thick blanket of white. It was a blizzard, and James and Avery had built their snow shelter just in time.

AVERY SLOWLY STIRRED WITHIN their refuge, blinking away the remnants of sleep. She found herself surprised by the warmth she woke to. Despite the harsh conditions outside, their improvised shelter had retained a somewhat cozy atmosphere. The pine-bough roof had served as an effective insulator against the winter chill.

She heard the crackling of a fire. Avery shifted, her eyes adjusting to the dim light within the trench. James knelt on the snow near the shelter's opening, feeding sticks into a small fire.

"Was I out the whole night?" Avery asked as she dragged herself out of the shelter.

"You must have been," James said. "I just let you sleep."

"I can't even remember when I fell asleep," Avery said as she took off her gloves and held her hands over the fire. “I remember thinking we were going to freeze.”

“Nature always has its way of surprising us,” said James. “We’ve got a new day ahead of us.”

“What do we need to do?” asked Avery.

“Get warm and then we’ll dig into our freeze-dried meal packages,” James said. “Then we’ll start making our way back to the truck.”

The morning sun gradually ascended, casting its golden light upon the snowy expanse and bringing warmth to the scene. James opened the freeze-dried chicken and rice meal in his pack. He took out a silver canister and filled it with snow before melting it over the fire. Then he poured the chicken and rice into the canister’s water to boil.

As they ate, they looked out over the vast expanse of the rugged mountains. Several feet of snow had fallen overnight, hiding most of the rocks and even some of the trees.

“THERE’S NO WAY WE can walk out of this,” James said as he finished his meal.

“What do you mean?” asked Avery.

“I mean, we’ll fall into the snow with every step we take,” James responded. “Snow will get into our boots, and in less than a mile, we’ll be exhausted and more dehydrated than if we were in the desert.”

“So…we’re just going to stay here?” Avery’s voice began to waver.

“No, we’re getting out of here,” said James. “With snowshoes.”

“Snowshoes?”

"Just follow my lead."

James explained to Avery that they needed to gather sturdy, flexible pine branches with lush, green needles. They needed multiple branches to distribute their weight. James demonstrated the technique, skillfully intertwining the branches with a paracord he kept in his pack. Avery followed along, her fingers working the paracord through the boughs in a crisscross pattern to create what resembled a webbed framework.

As the snowshoes took shape, James explained the importance of distributing their weight to prevent sinking into the deep snow. The pine boughs, acting as a natural snowshoe surface, would provide the necessary buoyancy atop the snow.

"Like walking on water?" Avery quipped.

"Something like that," James said as he lashed the boughs together.

Avery marveled at the makeshift snowshoes' resourcefulness. Once they were ready, James secured them to their boots using the paracord. The snug fit ensured that they were stable, allowing James and Avery to walk atop the snow rather than sinking into its depths. The added surface area provided by the pine boughs better distributed their body weight, making their steps more manageable on the winter terrain.

The crunch of snow beneath their feet pierced the crisp mountain air as James and Avery descended the white slopes. Thankfully, they could make their way back to the truck a few hours later, where they could then phone Bonnie, who was relieved to tears to receive their call.

JAMES'S ABILITY TO READ the weather signs and recognize that a snowstorm was imminent, combined with his quick thinking and prompt action to build the fastest type of shelter in the snow (a snow trench), kept him and

Avery alive that night. To enable their descent the following morning, their makeshift snowshoes allowed them to traverse the snowy landscape without sinking into the snow, which saved them time and energy and also limited the risk of snow getting into their boots. As a result, James and Avery were able to ward off the risks of sustaining frostbite or becoming frozen. Most importantly, they were able to stay alive.

3

Gauntlet of the Grizzly

Brooks Range, Alaska

The Brooks Range in Alaska, located north of the Arctic Circle, presents a formidable tableau of rugged peaks and rolling tundra valleys. Its very existence reminds us of how untamed the North remains.

Henry had ventured deep into the wilderness in pursuit of the elusive arctic grizzlies that roamed here. The Grizzlies of Brooks Range were known to be much larger than their counterparts in southern regions and were almost as big as polar bears. They were prized by the hunters who ventured this far north.

It was early September, and the snow had yet to set in for the year. That was perfect for hunting season, as Henry avoided spending too much time trudging his way through deep snow.

He was only twenty years old, but Henry was mature enough that the other hunters in his party permitted him to walk out of their camp alone. His uncle, Vernon, told him to hike a couple of miles towards the mountain's base where they could link up with their hunting buddies George and Jeffrey, according to the waypoint on their Garmin GPS devices.

Vernon assured Henry that he shouldn't see any bears en route to the waypoint. Most of the animals had been spotted farther up at higher elevations.

Even though he had a palpable camaraderie with his uncle and friends, Henry also yearned to spend as much time alone in the wild as possible. While the thrill of the hunt and the chance to shoot a bear or a moose drew him and his uncle up north from Anchorage each year, Henry looked forward to the opportunity to be alone in nature.

As he walked towards the waypoint location and scanned his surroundings, Henry deeply revered the untamed land. He imagined what it would have been like thousands of years ago when there were no cities and the whole world was as unspoiled as the ancient tundra that sprawled before him. This land most likely looked exactly the same as it did then.

HENRY CAME TO A stop by a mound and kneeled to rest. He set down his Remington .300 Win Mag next to him. He tried to visualize what it might look like if a city were built over the tundra, but the thought created an uneasiness in his stomach. This land was too beautiful to have the dirt torn up and buildings and roads installed. It was idyllic the way it was.

The wind picked up and a chill reverberated down Henry's spine. But the chill was not from the wind itself; Henry felt he was not alone.

Henry swiveled his neck to look in all directions. His alert gaze was drawn to a subtle movement in the distance, and his eyes widened with awe. There, a large distance away yet unmistakably imposing, was a grizzly bear.

THE GRIZZLY, ITS FUR a mix of brownish tones against the backdrop of the red and green tundra, exuded a formidable presence with its energy alone. The animal stood on its hind legs, surveying its surroundings with quiet authority.

Henry's heart skipped a couple of beats and then began to pound firmly against his chest. Even though the bear was far away, perhaps a hundred yards, it felt much closer.

"Just stay still," Henry whispered under his breath, repeating Vernon's words on what to do if he ever came face-to-face with a bear.

The bear was still on its hind legs, turning its neck left and right to survey its domain. Then, it suddenly stopped and looked directly at Henry.

Time seemed to freeze. Henry felt himself and the grizzly locking eyes even though they were far apart. For a second, Henry couldn't tell whether the bear would challenge or silently acknowledge him.

The bear slowly lowered itself onto all fours and remained still.

SUDDENLY, WITH A SHOCKING display of speed and agility, the grizzly surged towards Henry in a blur of fur and muscle!

For exactly one second, Henry was frozen as he processed what was happening. His mind remembered that bears were much faster than they looked. He remembered Vernon mentioning to him once that an adult brown bear could cover a hundred yards at full speed in less than ten seconds.

The second after that, Henry instinctively reached for his rifle. He had heard the advice of remaining still just before an imminent bear attack, but seeing the beast charge directly for him made him change his mind.

His hands shook, and when Henry attempted to pick up the rifle, the cold metal slipped between his fingers. The seconds ticked by as Henry reached down again to pick up the weapon with two hands and flick off the safety.

But time was not forgiving, as the bear had closed the distance with remarkable speed. It was getting bigger and bigger as it closed in on Henry with its teeth bared.

In a desperate attempt to defend himself, Henry didn't even bother to check if the rifle was chambered. He had loaded and chambered it after he had left camp, and there was no time to check again. He brought the rifle to his shoulder, aimed in the general direction of the bear, and fired off a single round.

The heavy recoil of the .300 Win Mag pounded against Henry's shoulder, followed by the deafening crack that echoed across the tundra.

HENRY THOUGHT THE BULLET had struck the grizzly somewhere in the shoulder, but the bear didn't falter. When his hand moved towards the bolt to chamber a second round, the bear was on him and tackled him to the ground.

The world became a chaotic blur as the clouds in the sky and the earth below met in a dance. Henry, now pinned beneath the powerful force of the grizzly, struggled to comprehend the reality of the encounter even as it happened. His face was pinned into the damp earth under the bear's massive paw while its fur enveloped him like a heavy blanket.

The grizzly, fueled by instinct and the gunshot's pain, swiped its massive claws through the air. The claws ripped through Henry's coat and flannel shirt and found their mark on his flesh.

Henry bit his tongue in an attempt to stop himself from screaming even as the pain seared. He had learned something else from Vernon: play dead and don't scream or move when a bear attacks you.

The bear raked him twice more across the back, and each time, Henry grimaced to force himself not to scream, staying as still as he could. The bear opened its mouth and sank its sharp and powerful teeth into the layers of clothing and flesh over Henry's shoulder, tearing through the fabric like paper.

Don't scream. Don't scream. Don't scream.

Finally, the bear let Henry go. It continued to paw him and try to move him, almost as if it were playing with him like how a dog plays with its toys.

Don't scream. Stay still. Don't scream. Stay still.

Henry repeated those words over and over again, even as he bled profusely.

To his relief, the bear started to leave him alone. Perhaps it was satiated by its display of dominance or just lost interest in the still carcass that Henry was pretending to be.

The bear stood momentarily, overlooking the terrain again as if nothing had happened. Then it disengaged from Henry completely, who continued to stay still, keeping his eyes open as he watched the bear saunter away.

Henry began to move only once the bear had become a speck in the distance. He had read reports of other bear attacks where people being attacked would play dead and succeed in getting the bear to lose interest, only to infuriate it and cause the attacks to resume once they stood back up.

Henry rolled onto his good shoulder and pulled himself up until he sat. The most considerable pain was in his shoulder where the bear had bitten him, but when he sat up, the pain from the claw rakes across his back became more pronounced.

With his hands trembling, Henry allowed the severity of his injuries to sink in. The bite mark on his shoulder throbbed with pain, and the three claw rakes across his back pulsed in rhythm with his heartbeat. Despite the pain, he knew that attending to his wounds was crucial for his survival, lest he bleed out.

While he had no pack in an attempt to travel light, Henry kept all of his items in his coat and pants pockets. He had a bandana, spare bullets for his rifle, and a knife, but now he was kicking himself for not packing a first aid kit. Henry had always told himself he would be careful and never sustain an accident as part of his justification for traveling lighter, but that was a decision he now regretted.

USING HIS GOOD ARM, Henry managed to remove his coat, the entire back of which was ripped open and bloodied from the bear's attack.

Then he drew his knife from the sheath on his belt. Using shreds of fabric torn from his coat, Henry fashioned makeshift bandages. He took his canteen and poured a little water over his shoulder where his flesh had been torn open and exposed.

Satisfied that the water would cleanse his wound to prevent infection from germs in the dirt or debris, Henry began to wrap the makeshift bandages around his shoulder and back to seal off the wound.

The gashes across his back would be harder for him to reach, but Henry knew he had to cover them to prevent infection. He tied the arms of his coat around his torso so that the rest of the coat covered the wounds on his back.

Once his injuries were attended to, Henry turned his attention to getting rescued. He was deliberately controlling his breathing, which helped him to stay calm. That was another survival technique Vernon had taught him, who explained that consciously regulating one's breathing was the best thing to remain calm and think clearly in any emergency.

HENRY SEARCHED FOR HIS GPS device, which doubled as a radio. He could call Uncle Vernon for help right now, but his heart sank as he realized that the device's screen was cracked and distorted beyond use. The device must have been flung from his pocket and stomped under the grizzly's paws.

Henry re-assessed his options. Even though he was supposed to meet Vernon and their friends at the waypoint, he could not know where that was since his GPS was destroyed. And with no other way of getting in touch with Vernon or anyone else, Henry realized his best option would be to return to camp.

Once there, he could acquire more bandages and gauze pads from the first aid kits they kept there. When he failed to arrive at the designated waypoint, Vernon and the others would know that something went wrong and would return to camp for him. Vernon had often advised Henry to do so in any wilderness emergency where he couldn't summon help: return to base camp and wait for him there.

Henry checked that the rifle was unchambered, then used it as a walking stick by placing the stock of the rifle into the ground and aiming the muzzle upward. He began to limp back to camp slowly.

The bite mark on his shoulder and the claw rakes across his back inflicted a continuous, throbbing pain. He adopted a slow and measured pace to keep the discomfort at bay. He held his wounded arm as motionless as he could, and he found he could minimize the pain in his back if he kept his back straight as he stumbled forward.

Leaning on his rifle as an improvised walking stick, Henry strategically distributed his weight to minimize the strain on his injured shoulder and back. Despite being fully conscious of the pain, he regulated his movements by walking slowly and avoiding sudden jolts that could exacerbate the wounds. The whole time, he continued to pace his breathing in a controlled fashion, with each inhalation and exhalation being deliberate to keep his mind calm. This mental fortitude and physical discipline enabled him to endure the pain during his arduous journey back to the camp.

Henry periodically took small sips from his water canteen. He would stop to rest quickly, take a sip, and then resume. He knew full well that the loss of blood and physical exertion from his encounter had increased his body's demand for fluids. He wasn't particularly thirsty, but hydration was a lifeline for him to stay awake and ensure his body would function adequately to carry him home.

Multiple times, Henry wanted to lie down on the ground and pass out, but he knew that would be the worst thing he could do. It would leave him exposed to the elements and perhaps to another bear. And if he remained asleep until darkness fell, it would be even more challenging for him to make his way back. He needed to return to camp before nightfall.

Henry could navigate by memory. Even though the tundra landscape was vast and seemingly uniform, it held subtle clues Henry had keenly observed during the initial expedition. Vernon had always instructed him to take 'mental photos' of different objects or patterns of the land so he could walk back to camp from memory. So Henry had been taking mental notes of the natural landmarks after setting off from the camp, and seeing the same landmarks again on his return walk gave him comfort and encouraged him to press on.

When Henry staggered into the camp, he collapsed to his knees and caught himself from falling forward with his good arm. He picked himself up and staggered to the main tent, where he hurriedly unzipped the entrance and stepped inside.

Inside were four sleeping cots, folding chairs, the wood stove, firewood stack, and the kitchen area with the camping stove, folding table, and propane tank.

Typically, Henry would peek into the stove and feed it more wood, but the situation was too urgent. He spotted the spare GPS radio that Vernon always kept among the kitchen supplies.

Switching the radio on, Henry dialed it into Vernon's frequency.

"Uncle Vernon?" Henry managed to gasp out into the radio.

Henry gently allowed himself to collapse onto one of the cots, laying down on his side not to disturb his shoulder or back wounds; he gently pulled a blanket over him. He was already making the cot a bloody mess, but he didn't care about that now.

"Uncle Vernon, are you there?" Henry said again through gritted teeth.

"Henry, is that you?" Vernon's fuzzy voice finally came through on the other end. "We couldn't get a hold of you. Are you okay?"

"I'm okay," Henry said. "But I think you guys should return to camp as soon as possible...I'm going to need a lift to the hospital."

HENRY DID A LOT of things correctly to stay alive. First, by shooting the accelerating Grizzly, he demonstrated the adage attributed to Mark Twain, "Courage is not the lack of fear. It is acting despite it." After being attacked, he lay as still as possible and 'played dead,' silently suffering through the pain as the beast ravaged him. Thus, he was able to shorten the duration of the attack. Had Henry continued to resist or fight back, the bear would have most likely pressed its attack and inflicted even more severe injuries on him.

Henry was also wise to wait until the bear had left before picking himself back up and tending to his injuries. Perhaps the most impactful thing

Henry did to contribute to his survival, besides immediately covering his injuries to reduce the bleeding, was to remain calm by controlling his breathing.

As a result, Henry decided to return to camp, where he knew he could contact the other members of his hunting party, who could then call for help. Making mental notes of the landscape as he hiked out (so that he could find his way back) also significantly reduced the time it took him to return to camp.

As Henry learned first-hand (or first-paw), confronting a grizzly is no laughing matter. But by keeping himself calm, he made wise decisions and made it back to camp alive.

4

Desert Venom

Mojave Desert, Utah

The sun cast a lengthy shadow over his figure as Jeremy walked forward.

With its rugged terrain and vast, open spaces, the Mojave Desert was the site of Jeremy's annual fall hunt for pronghorn. He admired the breathtaking backdrop of rolling dunes, craggy rock formations, and expansive sky that transitioned through hues of deep purple and orange as the day unfolded.

It wasn't even eight o'clock, and the temperature outside was already climbing past eighty degrees, with not a cloud in the sky. But the sweltering heat was of no concern to Jeremy, for he had grown up in the desert and was accustomed to it.

WEARING A WIDE-BRIMMED FEDORA hat and dressed in desert-toned hunting clothes, Jeremy blended seamlessly with his surroundings, almost like a small, moving part of the landscape. He wore a well-worn and dusty backpack with essentials for survival, including a hydration bladder filled with water, a first aid kit, granola bars, water filter and purification tablets, matches, and sunscreen.

He cradled his trusty Browning 7mm Magnum hunting rifle like a child. It was almost an extension of his body; its blued finish was worn, and its wooden stock and forend were nicked and scratched from years of use.

As he approached a ridge, Jeremy's eyes scanned the horizon for any movement. The pronghorn, with their keen senses, were very elusive creatures. Jeremy was fully aware that patience, as well as a sharp observation on his part, would be the keys to bagging an 'antelope' (as the pronghorn were colloquially known as) on this trip.

His gaze shifted to the ground, and there, partially buried in the desert sand, was a man-made object. Curious, Jeremy brushed away the loose soil with his fingers, unearthing a weathered yet beautifully crafted pottery shard adorned with intricate patterns and symbols that appeared to be of Native American origin.

The artifact seemed to echo stories of a past historical era, and Jeremy marveled at the craftsmanship. The pattern appeared to be a serpentine coil with elegant curves and intricate detailing. Jeremy recognized the snakes as a common motif in Native American symbolism, representing transformation and regeneration, the cyclical nature of life. The intricacy with which the serpent was drawn and colored hinted at the artist's skill.

SUDDENLY, A GLINT OF movement caught his eye, and he froze. A small herd of pronghorn grazed in the distance, their tan and white coats effectively disguising their frames against the desert palette. He would have missed them entirely if he hadn't seen them move since he had been enchanted with the pottery.

Jeremy placed the pottery piece into his pocket and crouched low, using the landscape's natural contours to conceal himself. He brought the stock of his rifle to his shoulder and rested the barrel against his knee.

Then he raised his GPS radio, clipped on his belt, to his lips.

"Sam, I've got a small herd about two hundred yards southeast of my position," Jeremy whispered into the radio. "Looks like we might have some action soon. Please see my coordinates."

There was a brief silence before Sam's voice crackled on the other end. "Copy that, Jeremy. I'm on my way. Hold tight."

Sam was his hunting buddy. About a mile and a half back, they had parked their Toyota Tacoma pickup truck and set off into the desert in different directions, intending to make an oval shape and connect by a river two miles away.

Jeremy remained still, his focus unwavering as he observed the pronghorn. The wind whispered through the desert, carrying his scent away from the herd. He adjusted the brim of his hat to shield his eyes from the sun. The intensity was building not only from the sun's increased heat but also from the anticipation of having a successful hunt.

As he continued to study the pronghorn and wait for Sam, a subtle but unmistakable rattling noise interrupted the whisper of the wind, sending a chilly shiver down Jeremy's spine.

Jeremy slowly turned, and there, coiled among the dry brush and sun-bleached rocks, was a rattlesnake. It lay partly under some brush, seeking relief from the sun, with its diamond-patterned scales appearing as the desert floor. Jeremy knew the reptile's unmistakable rattle was a warning that he had unintentionally trespassed into its territory.

Jeremy took a cautious step backward, his eyes locked onto the snake. He didn't notice the skittish pronghorn scattering in the distance, having sensed danger.

The rattlesnake remained coiled, but its eyes fixated on Jeremy as it flicked out its tongue. Sweat dripped down Jeremy's forehead as he contemplated his next move. Slowly, he began to retreat, carefully placing one foot behind the other.

The rattlesnake, however, had other plans. In a swift and unexpected motion, it lunged out of the brush and struck Jeremy's lower right leg!

A sharp pain shot through Jeremy's leg and up his body as he stumbled backward, clutching his leg and dropping his rifle into the dirt. The snake's fangs had pierced his pants and embedded themselves briefly into the flesh of his calf before releasing their potent venom.

Jeremy yelled out and fell to the ground. He scrambled several yards away as the snake retreated into its brush, its tail still rattling.

Once he was confident the snake would not strike again and he had put enough distance between them, Jeremy took a minute to process what had just happened. His hands trembled as he withdrew his folding knife from his pocket, unfolded it, and then used it to slice his right pant leg open from the knee down.

Pain radiated from the fang marks and his leg quickly swelled. The reality of being alone in the vast Utah desert without immediate help sank in, and a sense of isolation intensified Jeremy's sudden desperation. But he knew he had to stay calm and take action.

He pulled his first aid kit from his backpack. Remembering the basic principles of treating snakebites, he began wrapping a compression bandage around the bite site. The makeshift bandage was tight enough to slow the lymphatic flow but not so tight as to cut off blood circulation.

Jeremy's mind raced through his survival training as he secured the bandage and taped it to ensure it remained held in place. He needed to immobilize the affected leg to prevent the venom from spreading further. He didn't have any wood to fashion a splint, but he kept his leg outstretched and as straight as possible. He knew cutting the bite open with a knife and then sucking out the venom like movies sometimes portray was the absolute worst thing he could do.

JEREMY STARTED TO FEEL the effects of the venom. A feeling of nausea washed over him in waves, and his vision intermittently altered between normal and blurring. Fear gnawed at him from the inside out, but he fought to maintain composure. Panicking would only worsen his situation.

Fighting through the pain, Jeremy reached for his belt. His fingers fumbled until they closed around his GPS device. With a shaky hand, he powered it on and pulled it close to him, watching the screen illuminate with the coordinates of his current location.

"Sam, this is Jeremy," he rasped, the urgency evident in his voice. "A rattlesnake has bitten me. I need help. You have my coordinates, right?"

Static crackled on the other end before Sam's concerned voice responded, "Jeremy, stay with me. I've got your signal. I'm on my way. Just hang in there. You're not alone."

"Thank you," Jeremy managed to say. "I'm going to need help walking out of here."

"I'll contact nine-one-one on my phone if I get a signal," Sam said. "I'm coming to you."

Sam's reassurance was a lifeline, giving Jeremy a renewed surge of hope. But despair quickly displaced his hope as the snake's venom continued its insidious journey through his body. His nausea was so bad he felt like he was suffocating, which threatened to overpower his attempts at composing himself. The pain spread through his veins like fire, each heartbeat amplifying his agony.

JEREMY CHECKED HIS INJURY to ensure the compression bandage wrapped firmly above the bite was still in place. As he leaned over to check, another wave of dizziness swept over him. He knew the venom had already infiltrated his bloodstream, and while the compression bandage could help to slow the spread of the poison, he would need medical attention soon.

The scorching desert sun bore down on him, exacerbating the fever-like symptoms accompanying the snakebite. Drops of sweat trickled down his face, and Jeremy looked around for shade, where he could wait until Sam arrived. To his chagrin, there wasn't a tree in sight.

He pulled his bandana out of his pocket and poured water from his hydration bag over it before tying the dampened bandana around his head. This would provide him with at least some protection from the sun. He took intermittent sips from the bag to keep himself hydrated. The coolness of the water was the only relief he could feel.

Jeremy looked out over the desert, scanning in all directions for any sight of Sam. Shadows danced on the periphery of his vision, which he thought was Sam for a moment, only for the shadows to vanish soon. The landscape seemed to undulate like a mirage.

He considered getting up to walk out, but he knew walking would only increase his blood circulation and potentially facilitate the speed of the venom. It would be better to wait for help from medical professionals who could carry him out or to have Sam help him walk while he kept his leg immobilized as much as possible.

Jeremy sank back to the ground. He looked out over the horizon as the shadows at the edge of his vision returned, went away, and returned.

JEREMY REMEMBERED THE PIECE of Native American pottery he had found and pulled it out. He rested his head over a mound of dirt, using it as a pillow, and held up the piece of pottery, looking at the artwork of the coiled snake painted on its surface.

He couldn't help but shake his dizzy head at the irony. Had the pottery shard brought him such bad luck, or was it purely coincidental? Looking at the snake on the pottery, he couldn't help but imagine it was the same snake that had bitten his leg. If only he hadn't found and picked up the shard earlier.

Jeremy closed his eyes. As darkness took over his vision, he found himself surrounded by flickering shadows of dancing figures adorned in vibrant tribal attire. The rhythmic beat of drums echoed through the air, consistent with the pounding of his own heart. The earth beneath him felt sacred, and it seemed charged with energy.

He saw the silhouette of an American Indian priest emerging from the shifting sands, his eyes reflecting a profound wisdom. The priest approached him with deliberate steps, carrying a bundle of aromatic herbs that released a soothing fragrance into the air. As the figure drew closer, the desert sun cast a halo around his silhouette.

The figure spoke in a native language unknown to Jeremy, and the sand seemed to respond in waves, echoing the ancient incantations. Symbols and patterns danced in the air, swirling around Jeremy like spirits.

A sense of awe and serenity enveloped Jeremy, and for a moment, the throbbing pain of the snakebite was eclipsed.

"Jeremy."

Jeremy heard someone calling his name from somewhere distant.

"Jeremy?"

The voice called out again.

"Jeremy!"

Suddenly, his vision broke to pieces and Jeremy was thrust back into the reality of the harsh desert and the pulsating pain throughout his sweating body. The voice forming from the GPS device clutched in his hand reverted to its natural form.

"Jeremy!" the voice said again.

Jeremy realized now that it was Sam. His shaking arm managed to bring the GPS to his lips.

"Sam, Sam, I'm here," Jeremy spoke hoarsely.

"I see you, Jeremy!" Sam said. "I'm running over!"

Jeremy tilted his head upward. The familiar figure was, in fact, Sam running over to him, his rifle slung over his back and GPS in hand. He wasn't merely one of the shadow figures he had seen before.

Relieved, Jeremy sank his head back over the dirt mount and waited.

RATTLESNAKE BITES ARE RARELY immediately fatal, but they can be within two or three days if left untreated. In the meantime, victims feel an immediate, searing pain at the immediate site of the bite. Swelling will begin as the pain navigates its way around the body. In subsequent moments, intense feelings of nausea and perhaps even vomiting can occur, in addition to difficult breathing and intense sweating.

The best thing to do after sustaining a snakebite, as Jeremy did, is to remain calm while staying hydrated and keeping the site of the injury immobilized. Getting up to walk after sustaining a bite wound in the leg or lower extremities will only cause the venom to spread faster.

Jeremy was wise to have a hunting buddy whom he could call for help. Hunting out in the wilderness anywhere without having someone who knows where you are and who you can contact at a moment's notice is never wise. If Jeremy had been out there alone, or had he attempted to walk out, he very well could have perished that day.

After Sam came to Jeremy's aid, he could stand up while leaning against

Sam's shoulder. Keeping his bitten leg straight and off the ground, he hopped along with Sam's support for forty minutes until they reached an area with cell service, at which point they were able to call emergency rescue services for extraction and medical assistance.

5

Odyssey in the Everglades

Everglades, Florida

The Florida Everglades, a seemingly endless expanse of wetlands, presented a canvas of lush green vegetation, including tangled mangroves, cypress trees, murky waters, and sprawling prairies of sawgrass.

Sunlight filtered through the dense canopy of foliage above, casting shadows on the surface of the green and brown water below. The serpentine waterways, winding through the cypress and mangrove trees, could offer sanctuary or peril to those who dared to explore its depths.

When the Spanish conquistadors explored here more than five hundred years ago in the Age of Exploration, the Everglades protected them against several hostile tribes in the area. However, the region's inhospitable nature made it supremely difficult for them to survive, and they were forced to rely largely on staying in their boats just to sleep and stay dry. In some ways, hiding out in the wetlands of the Everglades was more dangerous than directly facing the tribes in open country.

NOAH MILLER AND JASPER Harrington thought of themselves as explorers as the conquistadors once were. While the two 20-year-old men were here for the thrill of archery hunting for wild hogs, which were primarily found in the areas of dry ground a couple of miles ahead, navigating the waterways in a sturdy yet weathered boat made them feel like explorers.

Their vessel was old and marked by the scars of countless journeys into these wetlands. It cut through the murky waters, the motor's hum blending with the birds chirping in the air.

Noah, with his sun-kissed skin and unruly dark hair, typically steered the boat, while Jasper, lanky and focused, scanned what lay ahead with a pair of binoculars.

"Nothing," Jasper said as he lowered the binoculars.

Noah nodded as the sunlight pierced through the canopy and carved directly into his face. He embodied the archetypal southern outdoorsman, and Jasper, while looking a bit more like city folk, was cut from the same cloth.

THE TWO YOUNG MEN have been inseparable since their early childhood days when they met in the third grade at elementary school. Noah was the son of a local wildlife conservationist and inherited his father's deep respect for nature. Growing up, he was always a natural navigator, the one who could read the stars and the winds and seemed to understand the wild that he was born with. Most of his time had been spent in Florida's humid swamps and forests. However, his father had taken him and his sisters on outdoor drips into the Arizona desert and Colorado Rockies, so he was well-accustomed to many different outdoor environments.

On the other hand, Jasper hailed from a family of archers who had passed down the art of bow hunting from generation to generation. He had never hunted with a firearm before, as the bow and arrow was his chosen weapon, and the Ka-Bar knife he always kept strapped to his thigh. His frame, lanky and agile, had strength acquired from years of hauling gear and traversing challenging terrains. Hunting was his greatest passion, and he was glad to spend this hunting trip with a trusted friend who shared his love for adventure.

Whether it was camping by the river, honing their marksmanship skills in the backyard (which mainly consisted of Jasper teaching Noah), or tracking wildlife through the vast Floridian marshes, their friendship had strengthened through their shared experiences and their abilities to live off the land had developed in the process.

As their formative years unfolded, the duo's outdoor pursuits evolved from childish escapades in the backyard to more sophisticated exploits in the woods and swamps. Even though their parents technically hadn't allowed them to venture out into the wild alone when they were younger, that never stopped Noah and Jasper from venturing out anyway on Fridays after school and during weekends.

This was their third official hog-hunting trip. It was becoming their tradition to head out once every three months when they both got time off work. Hog hunting in Florida was legal year-round as part of an effort to keep the population down, and Noah and Jasper were just two of many hunters in the state who took advantage of that policy.

Noah expertly steered the boat through the winding waterways, his eyes scanning ahead as he considered their next move to ensure they went around the trees that jutted out of the water rather than running into them. Jasper, his trusty bow close by, peered through his binoculars again, surveying the vast expanse of marshland.

"We're getting close to the dry ground," said Noah. "It's a couple of miles up ahead, I think. You know, the spot where the hogs like to gather."

"Sounds good," said Jasper as he adjusted his hat. "I'm ready to notch an arrow. These hogs won't know what hit 'em."

"Just be mindful," said Noah. "This isn't our backyard. We've got to find the right spot. It's not all dry land out here."

"Like we've never been through this before." Jasper grinned as he turned to look at Noah. "What's the plan?"

"We'll keep heading north." Noah pointed up ahead. "Somewhere where we can anchor the boat and move in quietly. The hogs always love the areas with some dry cover."

As Noah continued to navigate, Jasper reached into his pocket and withdrew a folded map that he spread out.

"Actually, just up ahead there should be an area of dry ground surrounded by water," he said. "That means there's fewer chances of the hogs catching wind of us. Might be worth checking out instead of the other spot. It's closer at least."

"Perfect," said Noah. "Let's head there. I've got a good feeling about it."

"Just one thing," said Jasper. "The dry ground may be nice for us, but it's also where alligators like to bask in the sun. We need to be cautious."

"Alligators?" Noah raised an eyebrow. "You don't think I'm aware? Seriously?"

"They blend in, man," Jasper reminded him. "You don't always see them. If we startle one, things could get dangerous. They swim fast."

"Alligators aren't that big of a deal," Noah said. "At least, they have never been for us before. If they turn out to be, this will be one wild expedition."

"If there's one thing I've learned after all these years, it's that nature never messes around," said Jasper. "Let's just find that dry ground and bag ourselves a hog, but remember, we're not the only predators out here. We're after the hogs, but the gators may be after us."

Their boat easily sliced through the water of the Everglades, leaving ripples in its wake as they drew nearer to the small island of dry ground Noah had pointed out on the map. The anticipation of the hunt hung in the air, and Jasper's fingers subtly flexed the grip of his compound bow by his side.

Suddenly, a sharp, unexpected impact rocked the boat! Both Noah and Jasper were jolted, nearly falling into the water.

"Whoa!" a startled Noah blurted.

"Did we hit something?" Jasper said as he looked around.

The boat was slowly listing to one side. Noah tried accelerating the engine, but the vessel refused to move forward. It was stuck!

"What's wrong?!" Noah yelled.

"Stop the engine!" Jasper yelled back as he bent over the front of the boat to identify the problem's source.

"See anything?" Noah asked, his voice wavering from worry.

Jasper's eyes caught sight of a puncture in the hull—a sharp piece of submerged rock sticking upwards had pierced the boat's aging wood.

"Breach!" Jasper exclaimed.

It was only then that Noah looked down and realized the boat was slowly flooding with water. He quickly assessed the situation. The water was seeping faster into the boat, and they couldn't salvage it. The archery equipment, their hunting packs, and the cooler with provisions were at risk of being submerged within seconds.

"Grab the bags!" Noah said. "Both of them."

The two men hurriedly picked up their backpacks and put them around their shoulders. Jasper's pack had his arrows lashed to the side, and he picked up the bow in his hands.

Noah's gaze shifted downward, punctuated by his slow realization that their boat was steadily succumbing to the swamp's embrace. The murky water crept in with a persistence that belied the vessel's aged resilience.

"The water's coming in too fast!" Noah said. "We have to get out. We can't salvage it."

"There has to be something we can do!" Jasper exclaimed.

"There isn't!" Noah said. "Get out!"

WITH A ALMOST SYNCHRONIZED jump, the two young men plunged into the waist-deep murky waters just as the boat surrendered to its inevitable fate, disappearing below the surface. The cooler, containing their carefully packed provisions, vanished into the depths, swallowed by the murky water.

Noah, now standing waist-deep in the swamp's embrace, observed the aftermath with a mixture of resignation and determination.

"What do we do?" Jasper asked, holding his bow above the water.

"We're heading back on foot," Noah said resolutely as he accepted the reality. "No other choice."

Jasper, still catching his breath, surveyed their surroundings.

"Can't we save the boat?" he asked with hope. "We can lift it back up and..."

"And what?" Noah interrupted. "It's gone, dude. That hole was so big and we had nothing to patch it up with."

"There has to be something we can do!" Jasper insisted.

"Well, there isn't!" Noah snapped back. "That old boat was nearly eighty years old and already had a couple of leaks that I was barely keeping patched. We have nothing that could fill that hole. It's done."

Jasper lowered his head as Noah looked around their surroundings. The swamp was stretched before them, its zigzagging waterways seemingly devoid of a clear path.

"But how do we navigate this swamp without the boat?" Jasper voiced the lingering question.

"We need to head south," Noah said with a heavy breath as he realized they now had a long journey ahead.

He took another moment to think before resuming.

"We need to head south," he repeated, his voice thickening with confidence. "Now, see that cypress tree over there?"

Noah pointed towards a towering cypress with exposed roots. "That's our first marker. We'll keep it on our right as we move."

Jasper nodded, his eyes following Noah's pointed finger.

NOAH CONTINUED, "AFTER THAT, we'll look for a cluster of lily pads forming a sort of natural raft that we passed by before. It's about a quarter mile from here. We'll walk our way towards that, keeping the cypress in sight. The lily pads will lead us towards a shallower part of the swamp."

Jasper shouldered his bow, listening intently as he tried to follow Noah's plan.

"Now, as we go, we'll look for a distinct bend in the water. It's like a gentle curve to the left, and it's marked by a partially submerged fallen log. That's our third marker. We'll keep the cypress tree and the lily pads in our sights as we navigate the bend."

He glanced at Jasper, ensuring the information sank in before proceeding.

"From there, it's mostly straight, but we'll need to be cautious," Noah continued. "The swamp floor can change suddenly. If we spot roots showing out of the water at a shallower area, we'll aim for that. As we progress, we'll keep our eyes peeled for a cluster of tall grasses on the right. That's the last marker. Once we reach there, we'll be close to dry ground."

"Do you remember each of these markers?" Jasper's voice was anything but confident.

"Yes, I remember each of them," said Noah. "I can lead us out of here. Just keep the bow ready and look for dry ground, okay?"

"Well, I guess you call yourself Noah the Navigator for a reason," Jasper said.

"I know the way," Noah said. "Now follow me."

The two men started wading their way through the swamp waters.

In one sense, Noah and Jasper's journey was the worst they had ever embarked on. They had passed the lily pads that Noah had mentioned earlier, but there was no dry ground in sight, and they were wading through water that could change rapidly from ankle-deep to shoulder-deep. Both men were soaked to the skin.

They both took long branches that they had broken off from the trees and used them as poles to feel their way in front of them to determine when the water's depth was about to rise or fall suddenly.

Additionally, both men had removed their boots (and socks) and lashed them around their necks by the shoelaces in an effort to dry them out. Jasper had been quick to remind Noah that the prospect of trench foot (when the tissue in their feet breaks down and results in possible infection) was now one of their greatest enemies and that they would need to keep their shoes and socks dry.

While going barefoot was unpleasant, wearing wet shoes while marching continuously through the swamp would be the number one factor that could result in trench foot. If it did set in, it would be devastating. It would be better to go barefoot for now and keep their shoes dry when they reach dry ground.

"How much longer?" Jasper asked after they had been wading forward for more than four hours.

Noah glanced up to the sky, realizing that darkness would descend in a mere two hours.

"We need to find a place to set up a shelter," he said urgently. "It's getting dark soon."

"You mean we're spending the night here?" Jasper asked.

"What choice do we have," said Noah with a shrug.

They found two sturdy cypress trees with branches high above the waterline.

"We'll make a shelter here," said Noah. "With no dry land, we must stay above the waterline, especially with night approaching."

THEY FASHIONED A FRAMEWORK between the two trees, forming a makeshift platform above the swamp water. This framework consisted of poles lashed with paracord, secured between two trees. Then they used the rest of the paracord to weave a chicken wire-style surface on which to lay.

They positioned their backpacks over the weaved paracord on opposite ends of the tree to serve as pillows. Finally, they secured large leaves and palm fronds, weaving them together to craft a softer surface atop the woven bedding base.

By the time their shelter was finished, it was dark, and Noah and Jasper were wrapping up their handiwork with flashlights in their mouths. Then they hoisted themselves onto the sturdy platform, leaning against their backpacks on opposite ends of the trees.

The air was chilly but not unbearable. Their boots and socks had also mostly dried out. Together, they lay there drinking water from their canteens and munching on an energy bar from their packs. They had three energy bars apiece, but each ate only one, so they would both have two more for the following day.

As fatigue set in, Noah and Jasper lay down on their backpacks, their eyes adjusting to the rhythm of the night. The sounds of the swamp became a lullaby, and the makeshift platform provided some comfort.

Slowly, they fell asleep.

NOAH AND JASPER RESUMED their journey the following day and continued wading through the swamp. They followed the leftward bend in the water and went by the partially submerged log Noah had mentioned.

Jasper's gaze shifted keenly across the water, his bow at the ready.

"Keep an eye out for any signs, Noah," he said. "Those gators don't announce themselves."

"We haven't seen any yet," Noah reminded him. "We should be good."

"They blend in well with the surroundings," Jasper retorted.

The thought seemed to startle Jasper, so he withdrew one of the arrows strapped to his pack and notched it into his bow.

"I think you're being paranoid," said Noah with a shrug. "The truck's parked less than a quarter mile away, I think. We'll be on dry ground in no time."

"If you say so," said Jasper as he kept his eyes peeled. "I just want to get out of here."

As they moved through the water, the swamp increasingly came alive with the subtle sounds of frog croaks, the buzz of insects, ripples from fish swimming underwater, and the occasional rustle of unseen creatures in the dense vegetation. The two advanced with a measured pace, their senses finely attuned to the noises.

After navigating through the water for some time, the swamp widened, revealing a larger expanse.

Noah pointed ahead, his voice low, "We're getting close to where the truck should be. This was roughly where we set off from."

"Good, let's keep it steady," said Jasper.

But little did they know, a congregation of alligators waited, barely visible above the waterline. Their eyes tracked the two hunters, viewing them as intruders.

Just one alligator would be enough to make any reasonable man worried. Each alligator was marked by a robust and armored frame and a broad, rounded snout filled with sharp teeth. Their dark green to nearly black coloration allowed them to integrate uniformly with the lush, watery surroundings. Their muscular tails allowed for efficient propulsion through the water. The consequences would be severe in the unfortunate event of an alligator bite. The reptile's massive jaw pressure could rip a man's arm off with a single snap and twist.

SLOWLY, THE SUBTLE CHANGE in the swamp's atmosphere became palpable. Noah and Jasper started slowing their pace as they felt the energy shift.

"Wait," said Noah. "Something's wrong."

The frog croaks started to die away. The ripples in the water became less pronounced. Insects no longer buzzed in the air.

Jasper whispered, "Be ready."

The two young men moved forward, the anticipation heightening with each step. A partially submerged log drifted into view as the river slowly carried it. Noah watched the log go by in an almost hypnotic state. Ripples in the water emanated from the log.

Then the log changed directions, shifting towards Jasper and Noah and increasing in speed. And to Noah's alarm, it was now moving *against* the drift of the water's current.

It was almost too late when it suddenly occurred to Noah that the log was not a log at all...but rather the dark brownish-black and scaly back of an alligator.

A second after Noah realized what was happening, the colossal alligator lunged out of the water with a thunderous splash! Its gaping jaws snapped shut just inches from where Jasper and Noah had been wading!

Jasper, adrenaline coursing through his veins, yelled, “Move, Noah, move!”

Without a second thought, they burst into a sprint, the water churned by their hurried escape. Behind them, the alligator surfaced, its eyes fixated on the fleeing prey.

Noah panted, “Keep going! Don’t look back!”

THE MEN ZIGZAGGED THROUGH the water, their every step fueled by the instinct for survival, but the water slowed them down.

The swamp became an obstacle course. As they ran through the water and avoided logs, Jasper glanced over his shoulder and shouted, “Where do we go, Noah?!”

Noah, his heart pounding, replied, “Just go straight! There should be higher ground just up ahead, and the truck will be there!”

Suddenly, Noah’s foot caught on a submerged root, sending him sprawling forward with a yelp of pain. He then fell face-first into the water with a massive splash. He winced as he came to the surface and clutched at his ankle.

Jasper, a few steps ahead, turned back in alarm.

“Noah! You alright?” Jasper called out.

Gritting his teeth, Noah pushed himself up. “Go, Jasper! I’ll catch up!”

Determination fueled his voice, but the pain in his ankle slowed his progress as he continued to limp forward. Noah realized he had most likely twisted it.

Jasper continued running forward, and gradually, the water became shallower and shallower. He stopped when he realized his legs were finally out of water entirely and he was standing over dry ground. As he caught his breath, he saw their pickup truck and trailer parked up ahead.

HE TURNED AROUND TO see that Noah was still limping in the shallow water. But narrowly behind Noah, another alligator appeared on the water's surface and was closing in fast!

"Noah, look out!" Jasper shouted.

In that split second, fear flashed in Noah's eyes as he turned to see the deadly reptile closing him, mere meters away!

Jasper instinctively raised his bow, swiftly notched an arrow, drew the drawstring back, and released it with precision.

The arrow sailed through the air, finding its mark on the alligator's side and halting its advance.

Seizing his chance, Noah scrambled forward, the adrenaline overpowering the pain in his ankle, until he collapsed onto the dry ground beside his friend.

The wounded alligator, the arrow sticking out of its side, turned and disappeared under the water.

Noah was on the ground, gasping for breath, beside Jasper, who had instinctively loaded another arrow into his bow.

"Thanks for having my back," Noah managed to say as he clutched his ankle.

As Jasper realized no more threat, he lowered the bow gradually.

Then he said the only thing he could think of: "Well, that was wild."

Noah and Jasper did several things right to ensure their survival, the most important of which was navigation. Swamps are wet, unforgiving, filled with nasty and dangerous creatures, and very difficult to navigate. Noah was very smart to keep note of landmarks as they traveled via boat through the swamps so they knew how to walk back. Had he not done that, they could probably have walked on endlessly, exhausting their food and water supplies.

Another thing they did right was elevate their shelter above the waterline and take action to keep their boots and socks dry by wrapping them around their necks to prevent the onset of trench foot.

Swamps are among the most challenging environments to survive in, especially when no dry areas of land are in sight. The most important thing you can do to aid in your survival while venturing into a swamp is to keep track of where you are going and make mental notes of various landmarks so you can trace your way back out.

6

Adrift in a Gray of Mist and Waves

Atlantic Ocean, off the coast of Massachusetts

As the sun ascended over the horizon, casting a golden glow upon the vast expanse of the Atlantic, Ethan sat at the helm of his weathered fishing rowboat, *The Siren's Call*. The same boat had carried him in countless fishing endeavors off the Massachusetts coast. With the salt-laden air filling his lungs, he surveyed the dance of the waves while setting his fishing lines over his poles.

Though a young fisherman at just nineteen years of age, Ethan was mature and well-seasoned by many years of fishing. The beige sand from the Massachusetts coastline stood resolute on the horizon, its silhouette promising familiarity and the bounty of a day's catch. Ethan's uncle, Jack, had always taught him never to leave the sight of the coastline so he would never become adrift at sea. Ethan strictly adhered to his rule as if it were a religion.

THE SIREN'S CALL WAS a modest craft that had been kissed by countless sunrises and was painted seafoam. It bobbed in harmony with the waves as if it were an extension of the ocean itself.

Ethan's journey to becoming a fisherman was a tragic one. He had been born in the heartland of Indiana and grew up in the woods with his friends and family, hunting for pheasant and deer. However, the tranquility of his childhood was shattered at the age of twelve with the untimely passing of his parents in a car accident.

Ethan was shocked when the police came to his door in the middle of the night to deliver the news. He was an only child, and it took several days for the reality of what had happened to set in. He was sent on a plane to Boston, where Jack picked him up. Ethan had only met Jack twice before, but no other close relatives were willing to take him in.

Jack was a construction worker and a seasoned fisherman, and he became a guardian and mentor in the art and craft of seafaring and fishing. The transition from the landlocked Indiana to the coastline of the Atlantic Ocean was transformative for Ethan. Though it took him years to settle in and develop a father-son relationship with his uncle, he found peace with fishing. It was the only thing that could keep his mind off the tragedy in Indiana and his struggle to fit in with the other kids in school. Ethan was alone on his boat fishing but felt most comfortable that way.

The small coastal town where he and Jack lived consisted of a harbor with an intricate maze of docks. *The Siren's Call* was always parked at Jack's rented boat slip on the dock. When Ethan turned eighteen, Jack allowed him to take the boat onto the ocean on his own for the first time, and again with the stipulation that Ethan was never to leave the sight of the coast.

It was only under Jack's continued guidance through the years that Ethan learned how the ocean worked, specifically how to read the currents, anticipate changing weather patterns, and read the subtle language of the waves. Ethan also learned how to mend nets, set fishing lines, and cast lines out into the sea.

IN THE PROCESS, JACK always entertained Ethan with sea folklore, telling tales of fishermen who spent their lives out there, some of whom were even claimed by the sea. Ethan's favorite story was about a fisherman named Elias, who was said to be a guardian of all the other fishermen who came after him in the area.

Elias was once a seasoned mariner from the early 1900s who had cast countless nets into the Atlantic off the same Massachusetts coast, only to meet an untimely end beneath the relentless currents in the middle of a storm.

Jack claimed that Elias's spirit found solace within the ocean, forever tethered to the waters he loved. In the quiet hours when the moonlit waves cast a silver-like glow upon the horizon, fishermen swore to have glimpsed the ghost of Elias or at least to have felt his presence in the middle of raging sea storms that they only barely survived. As the legend went, Elias watched over fishermen who navigated the same waters that once claimed him. Ethan was always looking for Elias, but he had yet to see him. Was it true or merely a legend?

ETHAN CONTEMPLATED THIS AS he worked on his net. As he did so, a subtle shroud began to materialize around him and *The Siren's Call*. A thick gray mist, almost as thick as breath in freezing temperatures, started to cover the boat.

Undeterred, Ethan continued his task. Once he finished with the net, he cast his line into the unknown with the confidence borne of familiarity. Yet, as the gray mist enveloped him, a growing unease settled in his stomach.

This will go away soon, Ethan told himself. *It has to.*

Ethan continued to cast his line into the mist. He hoped for at least a nibble, but the fish weren't biting.

About an hour later, the fog gradually lifted. Ethan looked up and saw gray clouds forming in the sky, covering up the sun that had previously been shining over him.

Ethan frantically looked around, but the coastline was nowhere in sight. The ocean extended its domain everywhere around him, forming an infinite circle around *The Siren's Call*.

As Ethan gazed at the vast horizon, the magnitude of his predicament started to sink in. He was a lone fisherman; his boat was a solitary vessel in a gray of mist and waves, and he didn't know how far he was from the coastline or which direction it was in.

It dawned on Ethan that he was adrift at sea.

IT TOOK ANOTHER HOUR for Ethan to realize that he needed to take action. He had stopped fishing, but he had hoped that the coastline would come back into view. It never did. The fog may have lifted, but Ethan felt more alone now than before.

Ethan decided the time had come to use the navigational skills Jack had taught him throughout their countless fishing trips. First, he observed the direction of the prevailing wind, which Jack had taught him was an essential indicator in maritime navigation. By feeling the breeze on his face, Ethan could figure out the direction from which it blew. He knew that the prevailing winds in this region often came from the west, carrying the scent of land out to sea. Therefore, heading west would be his safest bet to reach land.

Next, Ethan paid attention to the movement of the waves. The Atlantic, despite its unpredictable temperament, often bore subtle clues about how close land was. Jack had taught Ethan that the waves tended to build and break differently depending on their general proximity to the shoreline. Ethan scrutinized the pattern of the swells, noting any irregularities or changes that might signify an approaching coastline.

Closer to land, the waves tended to rise and peak in a more organized fashion, forming obvious, recognizable patterns. Conversely, in deeper waters further away from the coastline, the waves would exhibit a more unbridled and random nature, with less-defined peaks and troughs. The fact that the waves resembled the former was a clear clue to Ethan that the coastline had to be at least somewhat close.

The color of the water itself also offered insights. Coastal waters were heavily influenced by sediment, underwater terrain, and proximity to shore, often exhibiting variations in color as a result. Ethan leaned over the side of his rowboat and peered into the water, discerning shifts in hue that hinted at the underwater landscape beneath. He could tell that while he was farther from the coastline than he had been, he wasn't *that far*. That offered at least some degree of assurance.

THE SUN, A CELESTIAL guide in the vast maritime expanse, also played a crucial role. With a practiced eye, Ethan gauged the angle and position of the sun in the sky. Knowing the time of day, he could estimate his direction by considering the sun's trajectory across the sky.

Ethan took hold of both oars and began to row, following the westerly direction according to his compass.

But as his oar blades sliced through the water with determined strokes, a subtle shift in the atmosphere began to take shape. The once steady breeze was getting heavier. Ethan was wearing a jacket and long pants, but he was feeling chilly. The gray clouds darkened.

The prospect of rain was not exciting for Ethan, but he was prepared. He stopped rowing for a moment to put on his raincoat, which was long enough to cover his entire body. Jack insisted he always bring this item out when going fishing.

"Don't trust what the weatherman tells you," Jack had said. "Always be prepared."

Ethan continued to row, only to be startled by the distant rumble of thunder echoing across the ocean. Ethan knew that the sky's low growl was announcing the imminent arrival of a tempest.

Ethan's heart pounded against his chest. His eyes scanned the horizon, recognizing the telltale signs of an approaching storm. Dark, brooding clouds were gathering over him, creating a canopy that increasingly blocked out the sky. The atmospheric pressure shifted, and an unsettling stillness settled over the sea.

The waves began to swell and surge with increased restlessness by forces brewing underneath the surface. It was as if invisible beings from beneath the ocean were causing the waves to move.

Ethan quickened his pace with his oars, more desperate than ever to reach the coastline. He felt the first subtle droplets of rain, cool against his face. The distant thunder grew louder, bouncing off the ocean's surface.

IN THE DISTANCE, ETHAN could see that the once clear horizon was no longer flat as tumultuous white-capped waves rose and crashed with increasing ferocity. The sea had turned treacherous in the blink of an eye, and Ethan mentally prepared himself for the trial ahead.

If this was his day to die, then it was his day to die. He could only try his best to survive and hope that the ocean would spare him.

But the ocean didn't spare Elias, Ethan thought.

Would he become a new Elias, a new fisherman who was thrown into the sea and where legends would be formed about him? At least if he died today, he would be remembered somehow.

The rain intensified and the waves grew, rocking his rowboat up and down. As the storm bore down on Ethan and *The Siren's Call*, he took action using the same skills that Jack had taught him before.

First, he strapped on his life jacket over his raincoat and tightened it as far as he could. Then he adjusted the positioning of his rowboat relative to the oncoming waves, aiming to steer the boat at a slight angle to the oncoming swells. Jack had referred to this technique as "angling into the waves," allowing the rowboat to ride over the waves more smoothly, minimizing the risk of capsizing.

Ethan also remembered Jack teaching him the importance of maintaining a low center of gravity within the boat. He shifted his weight towards the center of the boat, adopting a low and stable posture with his hands grasping the oars tightly to reduce the odds of them falling out. This ensured better stability for the vessel, reducing the likelihood of it being overturned by the raging waves.

Ethan periodically bailed out excess water that splashed over the sides to further secure the boat's stability. Using a small bucket, another item Jack had insisted he should always bring with him without exception, he scooped out the infiltrating seawater to stop it from adding unnecessary weight to the vessel. Maintaining buoyancy was paramount in keeping the rowboat afloat amid the storm's onslaught.

The wind howled, the rain came down like a shower, and the waves were formidable. Ethan maintained a firm grip on the oars, using them for propulsion and as tools for steering and maintaining control. He strategically timed his strokes, synchronizing with the rhythm of the waves to navigate the turbulent waters more effectively.

SUDDENLY, WITH A DEAFENING roar, one large wave crested and crashed against *The Siren's Call,* throwing Ethan from the boat into the sea below! There was a whirl of gray clouds as Ethan released his grip from the oars and fell sideways before submerging in the churning sea.

But his survival instincts didn't leave him. Even underwater, he recalled the importance of remaining calm no matter what, just as Jack had told him. He expected the buoyancy from his life jacket to become his ally and propel him back to the surface, but it didn't.

To Ethan's horror, he felt around his torso and quickly realized that he had slipped out of the life jacket in the process of falling over! But he had tied it as tightly as he could have. How could it have slipped away?

It must have slid against the slippery surface of his rain jacket, Ethan thought as he thrashed about. He should have put the life jacket on first and his coat over it.

But he didn't give up. He knew from Jack that even amid a raging sea storm, the human body naturally possessed buoyant properties. He spread his limbs, creating surface area to minimize sinking, and focused on holding his breath.

As he fought to pull himself to the surface, an unexpected force seemed to guide him as if an unseen hand was pushing him up.

NOW AFLOAT IN THE storm-tossed sea, Ethan reached the surface and gasped for breath. Immediately, he looked around and located his rowboat amidst the chaotic waves. He remembered another crucial survival tactic Jack taught him — swimming parallel to the oncoming waves. By aligning himself with the wave direction, he could swim more efficiently as he stroked his way to the boat.

Ethan's training prevailed. He swam with measured strokes, and The Siren's Call grew closer with each determined effort. As he neared, Ethan reached for the boat's side, grabbed hold, and leveraged his remaining strength with both hands to hoist himself back on board.

Was it Elias who had helped him reach the surface? The thought crossed his mind as he worked to regain control of his rowboat by grabbing hold of both oars. Despite being soaked to the skin, Ethan again steered the boat at a slight angle to the oncoming waves while positioning himself at the center of the boat.

The waves began to relent, and the rain and wind slowed. Ethan's heart rate slowed with it. Looking above, he saw that the clouded sky was starting to unveil random patches of blue.

The rhythm of the waves, once a symphony of chaos, transitioned into a gentler dance. Taking advantage of the waning tempest, Ethan checked his compass to ensure he was still heading west. To his immense relief, he was.

A surreal calm settled over the sea. The air now carried the crisp freshness that followed a cleansing rain. The waves rolled with more subdued energy as if nature was catching its breath after the dramatic performance that had tested Ethan's resolve to survive in ways never before.

Ethan breathed a huge sigh of relief and allowed himself a moment of reflection. It was incredible to him how the ocean could change between calmness and a raging storm within moments. Perhaps it was the most unpredictable part of nature as a whole.

He glanced behind him, and to his relief, the Massachusetts shoreline was coming into view.

Falling back into his boat with his hands over his face, he prayed a prayer of gratitude to God that he had managed to come back to the surface after being thrown overboard and that his boat had managed to stay afloat in the process. He didn't know whether it was God or Elias who had propelled him to the surface when he was thrown into the waters, but either way, Ethan was just beyond glad to be alive.

He picked himself back up and began rowing towards the coastline.

THERE WERE MANY THINGS Ethan did right to survive, but the most important was navigation. Just like Noah and Jasper used their navigational skills to guide their way out of the swamp, Ethan used similar strategies to get back to land. However, whereas Noah and Jasper followed landmarks, Ethan used his knowledge of the sun, wave patterns, and winds to know which direction to go.

Had Ethan not possessed this knowledge, he would have likely rowed around in circles for days on end. This is precisely one of the reasons why many people stranded at sea can stay adrift for days or even weeks. The ocean looks precisely the same in all directions if there is no coastline within sight, and that's why it's so easy to get lost at sea.

Another thing Ethan did right was prepare his small rowboat for the increasingly large waves. By positioning himself in the middle of the boat, steering at a right angle to the waves, and continuously throwing water from the boat with the bucket, he could keep the boat afloat. And even though he was thrown overboard, he swam parallel to waves, which allowed him to be carried towards his boat rather than having to swim against the waves.

Ethan managed to survive that day based on his knowledge of maritime navigation and what to do when you are adrift at sea in a sea storm. Other people adrift at sea who lack this knowledge are not always so fortunate.

7

Echoes from the Caverns

Appalachian Mountains, Kentucky

The Appalachian Mountains, a majestic and ancient mountain range stretching over 2,000 miles along the eastern United States, are one of the most overlooked splendors of the country and the world.

Dense and almost mythical, the forests of the Appalachians are like America's Amazon. With green limbs outstretched, each tree contributes to the blanket over mountain slopes and hills. Rivers and streams carve pathways through the valleys and gorges, and certain summits seem to reach the heavens.

More than just a mountain range, the Appalachians are like breathing entities in their own right. They serve as a sanctuary for the white-tailed deer, black bears, mountain lions, foxes, and owls who call this beautiful place home.

HUNTER CLARKSON AND HIS newlywed wife Jennifer were happy also to call the Kentucky Appalachians their home.

Hunter, his name reflecting his affinity for hunting in the wilderness, possessed an almost spiritual connection with the land. His tousled brown hair and earth-toned eyes mirrored the hues of the forest itself, and the quiet confidence with which he moved proved how he could navigate the hidden trails and thickets. Clad in camouflage that seemed like an extension of the foliage, he moved with Jennifer by his side.

Jennifer was a spirited counterpart to her husband's serene demeanor. Her tall frame and ruffled blond hair contrasted with her husband's earthiness. A perpetual grin adorned her face, reflecting the sheer joy derived from the close, romantic bond they shared and the excitement in their pursuit of deer.

She had not hunted as much as Hunter had, who cradled a bow with a quiver of arrows over his back. Hunter had come to these hunting grounds countless times with his grandfather before he passed a couple of years ago. He knew these woods inside and out, so much that he never paid any attention to the map he kept stashed in his pack.

SUDDENLY, HUNTER FROZE, AND Jennifer stopped with him. Hunter crouched down, and Jennifer followed his lead.

Hunter pointed ahead, and Jennifer's eyes followed the direction to a majestic 7-point white-tailed buck grazing in a sunlit clearing. Her eyes widened in anticipation.

"Hunter, look at that!" Jennifer whispered, her voice barely audible amidst the rustle of leaves.

"I see him," Hunter replied in a hushed tone.

"Are you going to shoot?" she asked.

"Let's take it slow, Jen," Hunter said under his breath. "We don't want to spook him."

The pair stayed there almost breathless, observing the buck as it nibbled on the vegetation. It appeared to be alone with no does in sight.

Carefully, Hunter withdrew an arrow from his quiver and notched it into the drawstring of the bow, but he hadn't pulled it back or taken aim yet.

As if on cue, the white-tailed buck raised its head, its ears flicking at the subtlest sounds. Hunter held his breath. Was the buck aware of their presence?

A moment later, the buck turned and trotted off into the woods, disappearing into the foliage and shadows. Hunter and Jennifer exchanged a glance, the thrill of the encounter lingering in the air.

"We can't let him slip away," Jennifer murmured.

"We won't," Hunter said. "Let's move, but quietly."

The couple rose and moved forward, Jennifer a step or two behind Hunter. They both wore moccasins to minimize the chances of making noise by snapping a twig or crumpling leaves beneath their feet.

As they followed the buck's tracks, the forest gradually gave way to rockier terrain.

THEN HUNTER STOPPED AND crouched down again, and Jennifer did the same. Up ahead by a rocky hillside covered in big boulders, the buck was visible again near what appeared to be the hollow entrance to a cavern.

"Hunter, look," Jennifer whispered, her eyes widening at the sight of the cave. "I've never seen this before."

Hunter squinted and his brows furrowing as he tried to remember it.

"I don't recognize this place," he said. "We must be deeper than I thought."

Hunter notched the arrow into the bow again.

"I have a better shot this time," he said. "He's closer than before."

The couple exchanged glances, silently agreeing that the time had come to make the kill. Hunter slowly pulled the drawstring back and aimed. Jennifer's eyes widened.

But before Hunter could release the arrow, the buck turned and trotted away again...into the cave entrance!

"WHAT IN THE..." HUNTER said as he relaxed the drawstring.

Jennifer asked, "Did he just go into that cave? Should we follow?"

Hunter nodded with curiosity. "Let's go. But be careful."

Together, they approached the entrance to the cavern and felt the cool air that came from inside. Hunter notched the arrow back into his bow, anticipating the buck to be right there.

"You think he's there?" Jennifer whispered.

"I think so," Hunter whispered back. "Shine your flashlight."

Jennifer withdrew her flashlight from the pouch on her belt and switched it on. She shined it into the cave while Hunter pulled the drawstring back, ready to fire. They were disappointed to find the buck no longer there. Slowly, Hunter relaxed the arrow again.

"Where did he go?" Jennifer asked.

"I have no idea," Hunter said as he started to walk into the cave.

"What are you doing?!" Jennifer's eyes widened. "You're not going in there, are you?"

"Why not?" Hunter asked. "Come with me. He's gotta be in there somewhere."

TOGETHER, THE TWO ENTERED the cave with Hunter in the lead. As the cool darkness immersed them, they both used their flashlights to see that the entrance quickly gave way to a sprawling cavern system extending far beyond what the couple had anticipated.

Hunter ran his fingers along the cold, damp walls, his brow furrowed with wonder and uncertainty.

"I can't believe it," he said. "I've been coming here for years, and I've never seen this or anything like it."

Jennifer nodded in agreement, her eyes scanning the cavern's expanse. "It's like a hidden world beneath the forest."

As they ventured deeper, they found multiple paths leading in all directions. They chose a path and followed it, eventually coming to a large cavernous room with more pathways leading further away. Water dripped from the ceiling, and another rush of cool air shivered down both of their spines.

"The buck couldn't have come all the way here," Hunter said.

"You think he knew about this place?" Jennifer said. "I didn't think deer went into caves."

"I can't be sure," Hunter replied, his voice in awe as he shined his flashlight around to admire their subterranean world. "But let's keep moving."

"I think we've gone far enough," Jennifer hesitated.

"We know the way back, hun," Hunter said. "Don't be afraid. This is a once-in-a-lifetime opportunity to explore a place like this. What happens once they close it off and we can never return here?"

"Yeah, true," Jennifer said.

JENNIFER TOOK OUT HER phone and began to take photos as Hunter continued to walk towards the giant room in awe. The stalagmites rose like silent sentinels from the cave floor to the ceilings, formed by the slow accumulation of mineral deposits left behind as water dripped from the ceiling. The cones and columns of these stalagmites displayed an array of shapes and sizes, reflecting the diverse minerals in the underground water.

Meanwhile, above them, the stalactites hung like icicles from the cavern's ceiling. Each formation likewise began as a droplet of mineral-rich water that descended from above, leaving behind delicate layers of minerals.

Hunter couldn't help but view the stalagmites and stalactites as teeth, as if he and Jennifer had wandered into the mouth of a giant beast that could close around them. The thought unsettled him.

Suddenly, they heard a loud crash back near the cave entrance! They exchanged alarmed glances, their flashlights casting frantic shadows on the cave walls. The ground beneath them quivered.

"Hunter, what's happening?" Jennifer's voice trembled with uncertainty.

"I don't know, but we need to move!" Hunter's urgency cut through the growing noise. "Back to the entrance!"

As they retraced their steps through the twisting passages, the ominous rumbling intensified ahead. Loose pebbles skittered across the cavern floor, creating an unsettling, almost drum-like percussion.

They rounded the last corner, and to their horror, fallen rocks blocked the light from the cave's entrance!

"No!" Hunter screamed as he ran forward, releasing his grip on the bow.

Then the rumbling and crashing stopped. The entrance was filled entirely with large boulders.

"Hunter!" Jennifer scrambled.

THE ROCKS, DISLODGED FROM the hillside outside, formed an impenetrable barrier that blocked their way out. Hunter's flashlight revealed the daunting sight, and the reality of their predicament sank in.

"No, no, no!" was the only thing Hunter could say.

In vain, he pressed his entire body against the rocks to try to force them away, but it was useless. The stones weighed several tons each and there was nothing he could do.

"We're trapped!" Jennifer screamed. "Hunter, we're trapped down here!"

Hunter, grappling with the gravity of their situation, took a deep breath. "We'll find another way out. There must be other paths in this cave. We have to stay calm and think, babe."

He grabbed her and held her tight as she sobbed into his shoulder.

"It will be alright, it will be alright," he continued to assure her.

"We never should have come in here!" Jennifer sobbed.

"It's okay; there's always a way out," Hunter said. "Look at me, Jennifer."

Slowly, Jennifer pulled herself away to look at her husband through the light of their flashlights.

"There were other pathways in that big room," Hunter said. "We have to follow one of them."

IN THE DIM GLOW of their flashlights, Hunter and Jennifer retreated from the blocked entrance. As they returned to the cavern's central chamber, their beams illuminated the vastness of the underground space. The echoes of their footsteps seemed to magnify in the cavernous silence.

Hunter scanned the chamber, his flashlight revealing three distinct pathways leading away from the central area. Each passage was shrouded in darkness, and it was impossible to tell how far they led away...even if they led out at all.

"We have to choose one of these," Hunter said, his voice a steady anchor in the uncertainty.

Jennifer, her tear-streaked face determined, nodded in agreement. "Which one, Hunter?"

He studied each pathway, assessing their subtle differences. "Let's go with the middle one."

"Why?"

"It seems wider like it might lead to something. And if it doesn't, we'll return and try the other two."

The couple crossed the central chamber, avoiding the stalagmites that acted as sharp obstacles in their path, and entered the chosen middle passage. The narrow corridor extended before them, and the floor was rocky and uneven. The more they ventured down, the cooler the air grew, and the echoes of their footsteps reverberated louder.

Jennifer clutched Hunter's hand tightly.

"My bow!" Hunter suddenly stopped as he realized he had failed to pick up his bow after dropping it.

"It's okay, Hunter. Let's just get out of here," Jennifer said, her voice still on the verge of sobbing. "You can buy another one later."

Hunter hesitated for a moment. He held no sentimental value for the bow, and he had a couple of others back home. If he were alone, he would return for it, but he knew that venturing back the way they came would only terrify Jennifer further.

"Alright, let's move on," he said.

"Do you think this will lead us out?" she asked.

Hunter squeezed her hand reassuringly. "We can only hope. One step at a time, okay?"

THE PASSAGE WOUND DEEPER into the cave, branching into smaller alcoves and chambers along the way. The couple pressed forward on the main path, with Hunter insisting that veering off into the smaller chambers was only a surefire way to get lost. They were guided solely by the light of their flashlights.

The drip of water occasionally punctuated the eerie silence of the cave, but as they navigated the maze-like pathways, the distant murmur of an underground stream became more pronounced.

"Water!" Hunter said, and Jennifer suddenly realized just how thirsty she was.

They came to another small chamber with the pathway continuing onward and a small groundwater stream running. They knelt next to it and Hunter scooped his hand into the water.

"Is this safe to drink?" Jennifer asked.

"It's groundwater," Hunter responded. "It's cleaner than much of the water that rains out of the sky."

"Why's that?"

"The ground acts as a filter. Trust me, this stuff is safe to drink. Just drink it."

The two scooped water into their mouths until they had their fill. Hydrating felt good to both of them, and tasting the water offered some normality.

"Honey, I'm cold," Jennifer said, and Hunter realized she was shivering.

He held her close. "So am I."

"Can we get a fire going?" she asked. The idea of warming themselves over a small fire sounded like it would offer the same relief as the water. "I have matches and the kindling pile in my pack."

"No, absolutely not," Hunter said. "Starting a fire in a cave is the last thing we should do. The smoke will burn up our oxygen, and if it heats the ceiling enough...it could collapse right over us."

"What?!"

"We'll find our way out, Jennifer," he whispered as he held her again. "We have to believe that. Let's move on. These caverns don't go on forever."

THEY MOVED ON, AND the narrowing corridor led them through twists and turns, occasionally opening into small chambers on the side, but they still stuck to the main course. The darkness seemed to thicken around them. To save on the battery life of their flashlights (as they had no spares), Hunter had Jennifer shut off her light and stash it away. To ensure they didn't lose one another, she always clung to his hand.

Amidst the echoing silence, Hunter paused, his flashlight aimed at the uneven ground.

"Jennifer, check this out."

He crouched down and pointed to a series of small arrows scratched into the cave floor.

"Looks like someone marked this path before. Maybe explorers or spelunkers."

Jennifer examined the markings. "Arrows? Like a trail?"

"Exactly," Hunter affirmed. "It could be a guide left by someone else who was here. Let's follow them and see where they lead."

They embraced the newfound clue and followed the arrow markings along the cave floor. The subtle scratches acted like a trail of breadcrumbs, guiding them through the winding passages.

"How can you be so sure?" she asked.

Hunter explained as they continued to advance, "In cave exploration, people often use arrow symbols to mark paths and prevent others from getting lost. It's a way to navigate without natural light or clear landmarks. My grandpa taught me that."

Jennifer nodded, trusting Hunter's knowledge helping to alleviate the tension. "Smart."

"Cave systems are always a maze," Hunter mused. "But every maze has a way out. Trust me."

THE ARROWS LED THEM to a larger chamber with multiple exits. The couple paused, surveying their options. Jennifer pointed to an arrow indicating the leftmost path. "That way?"

Hunter followed the arrow's direction. "Let's trust the markings."

As Hunter and Jennifer followed the trail of arrows through the cave's winding passages, a subtle glow gradually illuminated the darkness ahead.

"Is that...daylight?!" Jennifer's voice rose in hope as she squinted into the growing glow.

Hunter's heart raced with anticipation. "I think so!"

As they emerged into a larger chamber, the source of the light became evident. A small opening in the cave wall revealed the light from the sun.

"We made it!" Hunter exclaimed, a mixture of relief and exhilaration in his voice.

The couple rushed toward the opening, and as they stepped into the embrace of the forest, the vibrant greenery and the warmth of sunlight enveloped them. The cave's confines gave way to the open expanse of the Kentucky Appalachians.

They embraced and held each other close.

"I love you, babe," Jennifer said. "You got us out!"

Hunter grinned.

"Team effort, hun," he said. "I bet we'll tell this story to our kids one day."

"Yeah, someday," Jennifer said.

Hunter turned back to face the woods.

"Well, I'm pretty sure we're at the other side of the hill now," he said. "Now we gotta find our way back to the truck."

"If we can find our way out of a cave, I think we can find our way out of a forest, too," Jennifer said, grinning.

Hunter reached into his pocket to pull out the map.

"Well, this will be the first time I've actually had to use this thing," he said.

Hand in hand, they ventured back into the forest in the direction Hunter believed they needed to go.

Hunter and Jennifer May have been a bit too adventurous entering the depths of an unknown cave system. As unlikely as the cave-in was, they can happen, and it's possible to be caught in the wrong place at the wrong time like they were. Numerous unexpected survival situations occur to people each year for this reason.

After they were trapped, Hunter and Jennifer did the only thing they could do: they followed the pathways and walked out. They were extremely fortunate that there were pathways leading away from that chamber; not all cave systems have more than one exit route.

Hunter and Jennifer were also smart enough not to light a fire inside the cave. Even though caverns can get very cold and wet, lighting a fire in an enclosed system like that can burn through oxygen quickly and possibly crack the walls under intense heat.

They had made it out, and they were alive.

8

Stranded on Safari

Zimbabwe, Africa

The African savanna stretched out like a panorama. Waves of grassy plains over rolling hills were dotted by sporadic acacia trees as far as the eye could see. The sky was crisp and bright blue, and the shining sun cast an orange glow over the landscape.

A herd of impala grazed leisurely on the tender grass. Each impala was dressed in a sleek, dappled coat and adorned with elegantly curved lyre-shaped horns. Impala were a common sight in Zimbabwe, with most herds like this one consisting of over fifty individuals.

Further off in the distance, three giraffes gracefully sauntered as they struck a contrast against the blue horizon. The impala herd paid them no attention.

RICHARD THORNTON BELIEVED IT was every hunter's dream to go hunting here in Africa at least once. Although he had been here for five days already, looking out over the savanna daily filled him with awe.

Richard was tall and stately and possessed an air of corporate sophistication that seemed out of place in the African wilderness. His neatly combed brown hair and trimmed beard hinted at his meticulousness, which served him well in the boardrooms.

Born and raised in New York City, Richard's journey into the heart of Africa was an unusual twist in his life's narrative. Growing up in a family where the concrete jungle was the norm, his exposure to the real jungle had been limited to the occasional family vacation in more domesticated natural reserves worldwide.

Only a few years ago did he decide to get into hunting. His grandfather and father had been hunters before him, but Richard had never gotten into the sport. When he turned twenty-eight, he decided it was time to give it a try. One guided hunt for white-tailed deer in upstate New

York was all it took to get him hooked. Many more hunting trips for white-tailed deer in New York and another guided hunt for red deer in the Scottish Highlands followed.

But his profession as a corporate manager had tethered him to the structured routines of office life, where decisions were made in meeting rooms. Whenever Richard needed to decide, he had colleagues and advisors who could help him.

That's why when he came to Africa to hunt, he knew he needed a guide—not only to show him around and lead him to the animals but also to help him make decisions along the way. Richard felt a little uneasy that he was constantly reliant on other people.

Richard had always harbored a latent curiosity for the wild despite his urban roots. This was kindled by tales he had heard from the other hunters in his family and from adventure novels and documentaries he viewed in his spare time, all sparking his imagination. However, the African savanna represented a level of wildness that transcended anything he had encountered before. As he adjusted the collar of his safari shirt, Richard couldn't help but feel a sense of vulnerability in the face of the vast and unpredictable landscape that awaited him.

RICHARD HAD A BIG Ruger M77 .375 H&H bolt-action rifle slung over his shoulder. He'd rented it from the local outfitter, and it was considered the minimum acceptable caliber for large, thick-skinned African game like the Cape buffalo.

His guide, Aidan Whitefield, had an identical rifle slung over his own shoulder, a big bore revolver of some sort strapped to his hip, and a pair of binoculars around his neck.

Richard flew to Zimbabwe six days ago, landing in Harare from New

York. This was the fifth and final hunting day of the trip with Aidan. He was picked up at the airport before being transported to the hunting lodge, where the outfitter rented him the rifle and treated him to a nice room and daily meals.

The following four days had seen Aidan guide Richard to a waterbuck, kudu, wildebeest, and zebra. The fifth and final day of the hunt was the grand finale: the chance to hunt and shoot the prized Cape buffalo.

When he arrived, Richard was surprised to learn that Cape buffalo were among the most dangerous African animals to hunt, even more so than lions. Unlike the solitary and more predictable nature of lion hunts, Cape buffalo hunts were fraught with a unique set of challenges. The collective defense mechanism of any buffalo herd was for each member to rally into a phalanx to protect themselves in the face of perceived threats. The massive size of each animal, coupled with powerful horns and sheer aggression at the slightest threat, rendered even a single buffalo a force to be reckoned with.

Their reputation as "the Black Death" stemmed not only from their physical prowess but also from the fact that they held grudges and were known to retaliate fiercely if one of their own was injured or killed. In other words, if one buffalo was brought down by a hunter, another buffalo in the vicinity may attack rather than flee. A full-grown male could weigh up to a ton, and when charging at full speeds, nothing could stop it other than an accurate rifle shot.

For a possible incident like this, Aidan was here to protect Richard from any dangerous buffalo who might become too aggressive. Richard contemplated canceling the hunt when he found out how risky and aggressive this species was, but the allure of being able to say he had shot one on his safari proved too great a temptation. His siblings and parents back home would never believe him. He just had to do it.

Aidan's weathered eyes, seasoned by more than three decades of navigating the African bush, detected a subtle movement within the dense brush. He raised his hand, signaling Richard to halt. The distant silhouette of a solitary Cape buffalo emerged, partially concealed in the shadows of the acacia trees.

"A bull," Aidan muttered, his voice barely audible.

They crouched down among the foliage. Although the buffalo have poor eyesight, the wind played a crucial role in concealing them from the animal's excellent sense of smell, and Aidan ensured they remained downwind to prevent the beast from catching their scent. He gestured for Richard to move closer to him.

With its massive horns and robust statue, the Cape buffalo grazed peacefully and was unaware of their arrival. Aidan motioned for Richard to chamber his rifle quietly, which he did. The tension in the air thickened as the duo assessed the distance and angles, calculating the best approach for a clean shot.

Silently, Aidan mouthed instructions to Richard, gesturing with his fingers to the ideal trajectory. They maintained a low profile, and the tall grass and brush gave them essential cover.

"Take the shot when you're ready," Aidan whispered.

Aidan readied his own rifle. He was prepared to shoot if Richard's shot missed or failed to bring the buffalo down.

Suddenly, the brush around forty meters to their right moved, and another Cape buffalo materialized from it and charged directly toward the two men, its hooves thundering over the ground!

Instinct kicked in, and Aidan and Richard raised their rifles, aiming for the charging behemoth. The sharp cracks of gunfire echoed, but the buffalo, fueled by pure adrenaline and its raw instinct to protect its territory, pressed undeterred. The initial shots, though precise, failed to halt its relentless charge.

"Run, Richard! Head for cover!" Aidan's urgent command cut through the air as he swiftly chambered another round into his weapon and returned it to his shoulder.

Richard obeyed, propelled by a surge of fear and survival instinct. He turned and sprinted for the nearest refuge, which was a sturdy tree surrounded by dense brush.

He dove behind the tree and heard Aidan's rifle bark again, the sharp report echoing.

Richard turned to see that Aidan was rechambering his rifle as the charging buffalo staggered, slowed down by the bullet impacts. The respite was fleeting, and Richard heard more thundering hooves.

The original buffalo they had spotted was also charging forward and closing in fast!

"Aidan!" he called out.

Richard raised his rifle and fired at the charging animal. He didn't know if he had missed, but regardless, it did nothing to stop the animal.

He couldn't believe what happened next. Aidan wheeled around and braced to take another shot at the animal, but the buffalo charged forward with unstoppable force. One moment, Aidan was standing there with the rifle raised to his shoulder, and the next, he was swept away in a blur of black and sent flying to the ground.

Richard rechambered the rifle again and brought it to his shoulder. It kicked ruthlessly against his shoulder and the crack of the gunshot echoed again. The buffalo, standing where Aidan had been, was hit. It staggered, turning its head almost as if to look where the shot had come from, and then collapsed to the ground in a cloud of dust.

Richard felt a lump in his throat. His rifle was empty, but he quickly reloaded it with the spare cartridges he had in his pocket.

“Aidan!” Richard called out. “Aidan?!”

Keeping the rifle at the ready, he cautiously approached the buffalo’s position. To his relief, the animal was lying still and lifeless. Looking around, he could see the other buffalo that Aidan had shot was also lying still.

“Aidan?!” Richard called out again as he frantically looked around for him.

Then Richard froze. The lump in his throat grew and swelled as if he had swallowed an apple.

Aidan was also on the ground, and he was lying just as still as the buffalo were.

RICHARD FELT GUILTY THAT he hadn’t buried Aidan. Even though he didn’t have a shovel, he wanted to dig into the earth with his bare hands and use a rock to help scoop the dirt away. He couldn’t stand the thought of leaving Aidan’s body alone, but it didn’t take long for two vultures to appear in the blue sky overhead.

And then in the distance, Richard saw a couple of jackals trotting over a hill, drawn by the smell of dead flesh. What would come next? Hyenas? Leopards? Lions?

Richard knew that many carnivores would be drawn to the site of the kills and that being anywhere close was the absolute last place he should be if he wanted to live. He only had so many bullets remaining and he couldn't protect himself with the rifle forever. So he resolved to put as much distance between himself and there and make it back to the hunting lodge where he could explain what had happened and hopefully recover Aidan's body.

An hour later, when he felt that he had put enough distance between himself and the site of the killings, Richard sat down to rest under the shade of an acacia tree. He took out his bandana, dampened it with water from his canteen, and pressed it to his forehead to help with the headache that was setting in from the sweltering heat.

He checked his phone. No service.

He wondered, "*Where am I even going?*"

It then dawned on Richard that he didn't know how to return to the lodge. He had been totally dependent on Aidan to guide him in and out.

As Richard sat under the acacia tree, grappling with the weight of his newfound isolation and the uncertainties ahead, a surge of vulnerability built up inside him unlike anything he had ever felt. The vastness of the savanna stretched out before him, but while it had been awe-inspiring, it now seemed terrifying.

With a deep breath, Richard forced himself to focus on the present. He knew that every passing moment increased the risk of encountering Africa's formidable predators such as lions or hyenas, and he also greatly feared encountering another buffalo.

The relentless African sun bore down on Richard as he thought about what to do next. He wished the sun would go away momentarily to spare him from the heat.

Wait, the sun! Richard suddenly remembered.

He suddenly remembered Aidan's guidance on the cardinal directions and how to use the sun as a compass. Their hunting lodge was located east of their direction, as Aidan knew they would be setting out west on this trip. The sun always rose in the east and set in the west.

Looking overhead, Richard could see that the sun had moved from its easterly position when he and Aidan had set off in the morning.

Driven by a newfound determination, Richard rose from his shaded refuge. He scanned the horizon, attempting to discern any landmarks that might guide him in the right direction. The savanna, however, offered little in terms of navigational cues.

Instead of dwelling on his uncertainty, Richard picked a direction eastward and began to walk, his rifle slung over his shoulder. The sun cast long shadows of him over the grass, and the weight of Aidan's absence and the ever-present threat of dangerous wildlife like the buffalo (or worse) weighed on Richard's mind every step of the way.

RICHARD SPENT THE NIGHT attempting to sleep in an acacia tree. It was midnight, according to his watch, but he had been unable to get anything resembling rest.

Richard strategically chose an acacia tree with low, sturdy branches for his nocturnal refuge. The elevation not only provided a measure of safety from potential ground-dwelling predators like lions or hyenas, but it also served as a barrier against the myriad of creepy crawlies that emerged at night.

During the day, Richard's thirst for water grew, and he drank mercilessly from the canteen, more than he should have. When it ran empty, he immediately searched for a new water source.

Richard knew that most of the time, groundwater was safe to drink. That was because the ground acted as a natural filter, but he also knew it could contain visible sediment that needed to be filtered out.

Upon spotting a shallow depression in the terrain, Richard used a small, improvised digging tool—a sharpened stick—to excavate the soil. Patiently, he waited for the water beneath the surface to collect, creating a rudimentary well.

He collected the water into his canteen and then folded his bandana three times over the opening of the canteen to act as a water filter. Tilting his head back and bringing the canteen to his lips, the water passed through the layers of the bandana into his mouth.

It was a risk, but one Richard was willing to take to remain hydrated and calm his headache. He had already lost a lot of water just from sweating under the sun.

THE NEXT MORNING, RICHARD continued his journey east. He had not gotten a minute of sleep the previous night, but he was grateful that he hadn't encountered any other wild animals and remained healthy.

He was growing increasingly concerned, however. He and Aidan had only walked for a few hours from the hunting lodge to get to where they were, but he had been walking for the remainder of the previous day and the current morning—and the lodge was still not in sight.

Was he going in the right direction?

He thought he was, but he wondered if he had overshot the lodge and if it was positioned somewhere to his north or south. He checked his phone repeatedly for service, but there was none each time.

But with each step, Richard's determination remained unyielding. He knew he only had two choices: to either keep walking and find a way out or die like Aidan had. To that end, he continued to trek across the savanna as the sun climbed higher in the sky.

THEN RICHARD STOPPED. OFF in the distance, he thought he heard the soft hum of a running vehicle. His ears perked like a dog's. Was it real, or was it just his imagination? His growling stomach and the intense heat of the sun were taking a toll on him and he had been getting progressively dizzier, so he couldn't be sure.

But the hum grew louder with each passing moment. His heart quickened as he strained to identify the source.

Peering across the landscape, Richard's eyes widened with a mixture of disbelief and hope. Emerging from the savanna's embrace was a welcomed sight—an approaching truck kicking up a trail of dust as it navigated the uneven terrain.

For a moment, Richard stood rooted to the spot, his eyes fixed on the vehicle drawing nearer. The realization that help was at hand filled him with gratitude and relief.

Unbeknownst to him, the other skilled guides at the lodge had set out in the morning to find him and Aidan when they had failed to return that night. They had sent out no less than three vehicles with separate rescue parties to cover a wide area to look for them.

Richard shouted and waved his bandana around in the air. He realized the truck must have spotted him before he spotted them because it was approaching him.

Exhausted but relieved, Richard collapsed to his knees. He had been found.

As MACABRE AS IT sounds, Richard made the right decision to flee from the site where the buffalo and Aidan died rather than burying his hunting guide on the spot. If more people had been present for protection, either burying Aidan or taking his body away would have been the right choice. But being on his own with no protection other than the handful of remaining bullets for his rifle, Richard was wise to put distance between himself and the site.

Even though he didn't keep precise track of where they had gone, he was also smart to remember that this hunting lodge was due east and that he could use the sun as a guide to know where east was. Additionally, he was wise to use his bandana as a water filter and to search for a damp area in the ground to dig for groundwater.

But perhaps the most important thing was that Richard had a rescue party who went out looking for him when he did not return the previous night. This is why it's always wise to inform someone of your intended locations so they can send for help if you don't return on schedule. In Richard's case, that method had practically the entire hunting lodge out looking for him.

When Richard returned to the hunting lodge, he informed everybody what had happened. Another party was dispatched to recover Aidan's body. Richard returned home a changed man. As he grieved for the loss of his hunting partner with whom he had forged a friendship over the few days they spent together in the untamed savanna, he also felt a profound sense of gratitude for his own survival.

9

Labyrinth of the Jungle

Peru, South America

The Amazon was a vast and enchanting expanse of greenery unlike anywhere else on Earth. Beneath the towering canopy, sunlight filtered through layer upon layer of large emerald leaves, casting an ethereal glow on the ground life below. Giant trees stood proud, their massive roots intertwined in an embrace. The air, thick with humidity, carried the fragrance of damp soil and the intoxicating scent of blooming flowers.

The sounds of the rainforest came alive with the cacophony of unseen creatures—from the jubilant trills of tropical birds to the haunting calls of howler monkeys echoing through the foliage. The ground was a mosaic of fallen leaves and vibrant undergrowth over mud.

In this emerald realm, biodiversity thrived. Exotic insects with iridescent wings fluttered through the air while vibrant butterflies danced in a kaleidoscope of colors. Stealthy jaguars, playful river otters, slimy anacondas, tranquil capybaras, and elusive anteaters all tended to their business, adding to the intricate tapestry of life in this lush refuge.

JAVIER ALVAREZ, ALONG WITH his companions, comprised a hunting party of four that had ventured into the heart of the Amazon, lured by the challenge of hunting wild boars in the primal depths of the rainforest. They had come to the same spot that they came to each May. Their single-shot rifles were slung over their shoulders as they trod lightly through the undergrowth.

Javier was a seasoned hunter with weathered features. He was a man of the jungle, having been raised in a small town about twenty miles away, and he and his friends had made countless ventures into the heart of the rainforest either on camping or hunting trips. He bore the mark of someone intimately familiar with the wild and more comfortable with it than the luxuries of urban living. His sharp and observant gaze closely surveyed the dense foliage before moving his sturdy frame forward.

As the hunting party pressed deeper into the Amazon's lush embrace, they arrived at a natural clearing bathed in sunlight, offering a brief respite from the dense undergrowth. The leader of the party, Sancho, held up his hand for them to stop.

"We'll rest here," Sancho said. "Twenty minutes or so."

The group sat down in the jungle, eating homemade snacks and drinking water they had brought.

One of Javier's companions in the party was Maria, his friend from childhood who regularly accompanied him into the jungle.

"The jungle has eyes," she said.

"As always," Javier responded.

Everyone in the party was sitting on the grass, but Javier was standing. He could still keep walking and he wasn't ready to take a break.

"And ears we cannot fathom," said Maria.

"We should keep going," Javier said. "The boar's area is still a good hour's walk ahead. We should get there as soon as possible."

"Let's not push our luck," Maria said. "We've already made good progress without any problems."

Juan, another member of the party, added, "Maria's right, Javier. The boar will be there when we get there."

Javier, however, remained undeterred, his eyes fixated on an unseen point beyond the clearing. "

"I sense something, my friends," he said. "There's a trail up ahead. I'll go a bit further to survey the area."

"You're going to go on without us?" Maria asked, bewildered.

"I won't go far," Javier promised. "I'll walk a bit and then wait for you. You'll follow the same trail, right?"

"We will," Sancho said. "But don't go far. It's not wise to split up."

"We're not splitting up," Javier insisted. "Think of it as just me scouting ahead a bit."

Maria exchanged a knowing look with Juan and Sancho, concern etched on her features. "Be cautious, Javier. The jungle doesn't always reveal its intentions."

"I know, I know," Javier reassured her. "I'll be careful."

JAVIER STRODE PURPOSEFULLY INTO the jungle. The air was so humid that it almost clung to his skin. The undergrowth crunched beneath his boots as he walked.

After traversing a modest distance, Javier halted, his senses tuned to the jungle's melodies. He decided to sit where he was and wait for Maria, Sancho, and Juan to show up later. For now, he could rest.

After about fifteen minutes, Javier called out.

"Maria? Juan? Sancho?"

His voice resonated through the thick air and foliage but was met only with silence.

"Maria? Juan? Sancho?"

A little fire of anxiety started to grow in Javier. He picked up his rifle and retraced his steps in search of the clearing where they had momentarily rested. However, the dense vegetation seemed to conspire against him. The familiar landmarks he had seen were no longer recognizable. He glanced at the trail and realized he couldn't recognize it either. Was it the same one he had walked?

"Maria! Juan! Sancho!" Javier called out again.

But again, there was only silence.

JAVIER FELT INSIDE HIS pockets. Besides the canteen strapped to his shoulder, he had a folding pocket knife, six spare shells for his single-shot rifle, and a box of matches.

Javier's heart quickened as he grappled with the disorienting reality that the rainforest had betrayed him. He could no longer recognize where he was, and he now faced the daunting task of navigating the labyrinthine jungle to either find his way out or reunite with the others.

He raised the rifle and fired a resounding shot into the thick canopy above. The sharp crack of the rifle shot reverberated through the rainforest.. He strained his ears, half-expecting the distant shouting of his comrades or another rifle shot to indicate where they were.

But there was nothing. Hastily, he ejected the spent cartridge, thumbed in a new one, snapped the action shut, and shot the rifle into the air again.

But it was the same result.

Javier lowered the rifle. He now had five bullets left, and he decided to save them for hunting or defense rather than use them for signaling again.

SUDDENLY, JAVIER TRIPPED ON a root he failed to notice and fell down a slight slope, losing his grip on his rifle. Though he managed to pick himself up, he felt a jolt of pain in his ankle and stumbled forward. He was unable to regain his footing and fell again.

A sharp, pulsating pain radiated from his lower leg. With a grimace, Javier gingerly probed the affected area, his fingers tracing the contours of the ankle in search of any irregularities. A subtle yet unmistakable swelling greeted his touch, accompanied by another surge of pain signaling that something was wrong.

He realized that the normal alignment of bones and joints had been disrupted and that he needed to treat this injury immediately.

Drawing upon the traditional knowledge shared by the indigenous community he had learned from, Javier identified medicinal plants with anti-inflammatory properties. He spotted a Cat's Claw plant, distinguished by its hooked thorns that resembled the claws of a cat, and known for its soothing and anti-inflammatory properties. Using his hands, he crushed the leaves to release their natural juices, which he mixed with a bit of water from his canteen in the palm of his hand, creating a rudimentary poultice. Javier gingerly applied it to his swollen ankle, and the cool moisture provided a little relief.

Next, Javier turned his attention to securing a makeshift splint to stabilize his injured foot. He scanned his immediate surroundings, then foraged for sturdy branches, selecting those with flexible yet resilient qualities. He was then able to fashion a primitive splint, placing two sticks on both sides of his foot and leg and binding them using vines that he cut free from trees with his knife.

JAVIER KNEW HE WOULD have to keep his limb immobilized to keep it from further swelling. Unable to walk out, his own way to survive would be to draw rescuers to him. He needed to build a fire to use as a signal for help and build an adequate shelter to prepare himself for the night. It could rain overnight, and he would need a shelter to keep himself dry.

He removed a lower branch from a tree to serve as a pole and used his knife to cut off the excessive branches. He would use this pole as a walking stick to take the weight off his injured foot as he moved about.

Then he promptly got to work crafting a shelter. He carefully surveyed the surroundings, searching for the ideal location, before choosing a spot with level ground.

Gathering long branches and flexible vines from the abundant vegetation around him, he began crafting a simple framework resembling a lean-to. He used his largest pole as the central support for the shelter, placing the end in the middle of a forked tree and placing the other end on the ground to form a slope.

Then he placed more poles he had collected against the primary pole to create a wall. He used a vine to secure the wall poles to the central pole, because otherwise, they could slip away under wind or the slightest pressure.

Then the time came to assemble the bedding and the roof. Javier collected large, flat leaves from nearby plants to create a waterproof roof. He interwove the stems of the leaves together, creating a tight thatch that would encourage water runoff and minimize leaks. He draped this thatch over the wall of the shelter.

Then he placed another layer of sticks and poles over the ground for the flooring and put a pile of leaves over the sticks. Javier knew he needed to separate himself from the damp ground as much as possible to stay warm and dry at night. The flooring he had created would not be nearly as nice as the bed he had back home, but it would keep him warm and dry and that's what mattered the most for his survival.

By the time Javier had finished the work, a good four hours had passed, and he knew dusk would soon be setting in. His attention now turned to building a fire.

He carefully selected a few dry leaves, cradling them in one hand while holding a match in the other. The match flared to life with a satisfying hiss, casting a warm glow on his face. With deliberate movements, he touched the flame to the dry leaves, which crackled and smoldered, gradually building into a flickering flame.

As the flames danced upward, Javier fed the flames with small twigs and dried branches, each addition intensifying the blaze. He planned to use the fire not only for warmth but also to signal for help.

He spent the next two hours gathering more fuel for the fire, being careful not to put more pressure on his foot. Drawing upon his knowledge of fire building, Javier knew he would need to create a fire with white smoke to signal for help. The fire would need to be large enough for the smoke to break through the canopy above.

Javier collected damp green leaves from plants with high moisture content. He arranged these leaves carefully, creating a small pit in the wet earth with a stick as a makeshift shovel. By placing the green foliage on the base of the fire pit, Javier ensured that the smoke produced would be thick and white so that it would be more visible from afar in the sky. Javier ignited the fire with dry twigs and leaves once the pit was prepared. The green leaves, with their moisture content, fueled a smoldering, slow-burning fire.

He had another pile of sticks and green leaves on standby to feed the fire continuously during the night.

Dusk was now in full swing as the sun prepared to set.

BEFORE SETTLING IN FOR the night, Javier decided to tend to one more task before he would allow his exhausted self some rest. Before, while he was building the shelter, he had noticed a guava tree, its slender branches laden with ripe, fragrant fruit. The guavas, resembling pale orbs with a subtle blush, dangled tantalizingly, just out of reach. Javier's heart quickened with the promise of a juicy and nourishing meal to help his growling stomach.

Drawing on the skills ingrained in his upbringing when he and his friends would bring down guava fruit, Javier assessed the tree's structure. He selected a sturdy vine nearby, its sinewy form indicative of strength. Tying one end securely around his wrist, he fashioned a makeshift lasso at the other end. He aimed for the base of the guava, threw it, and expertly looped the vine around its stem.

A gentle pull yielded a few ripe guava fruits. They tumbled to the ground, and Javier deftly caught one. Looking at it and the other fruits on the ground, he marveled at the bounty he had harvested. He considered it a gift of the rainforest and a reminder that despite how unforgiving it may seem, it would always provide him with everything he needed to make it out.

With that in mind, Javier collapsed onto his uncomfortable bed while munching on a guava fruit. The bedding was anything but luxurious and dug into his back, but he had a warm fire and a roof over his head for protection from rain. For that, he was grateful.

Javier was rescued the next morning. Maria had alerted the authorities that he was missing, and in the morning, a rescue party noticed the white smoke emanating from the thick jungle canopy. It didn't take them long afterward to locate Javier.

THAT NIGHT IN THE jungle was miserable for Javier. It rained hard, and his fire went out in the middle of the night. Even though the Amazon Rainforest is hot and humid, temperatures can drop when it rains. Being continuously soaked in water for hours on end puts you at risk of hypothermia, especially if you don't have warm clothing.

That's why the simple yet effective lean-to he built could have been what saved his life. It kept him dry, and even though the fire went out and he was cold and shivering all night, Javier could make it through with at least a couple of hours of sleep.

When he awoke again, he collected more green leaves to rebuild his fire. In anticipation of the rain, he had kept dried leaves and tinder under the shelter with him to ensure they remained dry. Striking a match, he relit the fire and added more kindling to fuel it before placing the green leaves in the depth of the pit under the kindling.

This was the fire that the rescue party detected a few hours later. By that afternoon, they had pinpointed Javier's location and helped him.

Javier should not have walked on his own into the jungle, but once he realized he was lost, he did many things correctly to ensure his survival.

Conclusion

While each of the stories herein is unique, they share one primary element in common: they reveal how human perseverance can be forged in the face of life-threatening adversity. I hope that you view these hunting survival stories as more than mere tales; I hope you learned from them and that you have been inspired to develop your set of essential wilderness survival skills.

Let's review some practical emergency coping skills that each of our characters applied to their specific survival scenario.

Of prime importance, they each remained calm and effectively made decisions to ensure their survival. After being thrown overboard into the water from his canoe and sustaining a concussion, Will promptly took decisive action to start a fire, build a shelter, and purify water. James and Avery recognized that a snowstorm was about to hit and promptly prepared an insulated snow shelter.

Henry knew better than to fight back against the Grizzly, played dead until it left, and then went directly back to the camp using the natural landmarks as a guide. Jeremy took immediate action to treat his snakebite wound and kept his leg immobilized while he waited for his buddy to rejoin him.

Noah and Jasper used their navigational skills to navigate through the swamp to return to the truck. Ethan used his navigational skills and knowledge of how to weather the storm to row his boat back towards the coastline and navigate through the massive waves. Hunter and Jennifer stayed calm as they meandered through the underground cavernous maze.

Richard took action to get away from the kill site and used directional sense to reason the location of his hunting lodge as he returned. Javier took immediate action to immobilize his leg, build a sturdy shelter to protect himself from rain and build a fire with white smoke to signal for help.

BASED ON THEIR SUCCESSFUL application of learned wilderness survival skills, I recommend the following skill sets to learn and practice.

1. Remain Calm Amid Adversity: Maintaining a composed mental focus is a fundamental survival skill in the face of adversity. Panic can cloud judgment and hinder decision-making. By seeking and maintaining emotional calm, we can think more clearly, assess our situation objectively, and make rational choices that contribute to our overall well-being and chances of survival. That is fundamentally what each character in our stories did to survive.

2. Learn Navigational Skills: Navigational skills are crucial for survival in the wilderness. Whether traversing dense jungles or trekking across open savannas, understanding how to read natural landmarks, use maps, and employ basic orientation tools is essential. Those with a solid grasp of navigation can find their way through unfamiliar terrain, increasing their chances of reaching safety. Noah in the swamp, Jeremy in the desert, Ethan in the ocean, and Richard in the cave all showed us how

knowing basic navigational skills can save your life.

3. Know How To Build a Shelter: The ability to construct a shelter from available resources is vital for protection against the elements, especially as we saw with Javier in the jungle. In various environments, from rainforests to open plains, creating a shelter that provides warmth, safety, and comfort is a crucial survival skill. Basic bushcraft knowledge helps individuals adapt to their surroundings and safeguards them from harsh and unpredictable conditions. Jeremy in the desert and James with Avery in the mountains showed us the importance of shelter-building for protection against harsh elements that could otherwise harm us.

4. Learn How To Build a Fire: Fire is a versatile and powerful survival tool, providing warmth, cooking capabilities, and a means of signaling for help. Understanding various fire-making techniques using natural resources and basic tools is essential. Those proficient in fire-making increase their chances of getting warm, preparing food, and attracting attention in emergencies. As Will showed us in the mountains, white smoke created by burning moist, green leaves is your best bet for signaling for help when you only have natural materials.

5. Know How To Purify Water: Clean water is also paramount for survival. Learning methods to purify water, such as boiling or using natural filtration systems, is crucial. Those skilled in water purification can ensure a safe and reliable supply, reducing the risk of waterborne illnesses and maintaining overall health in challenging environments. Sometimes the simplest solution is best, like Richard on safari when he dug for groundwater and then filtered it with his bandana, or Will in the mountains when he created his makeshift water filter out of entirely natural materials that he assembled in the riverside woods.

6. Identify Edible Plants: Knowledge of local flora and identifying edible plants are crucial for sourcing safe food in the wild. Whether exploring rainforests or navigating savannas, understanding which plants are safe to eat ensures a sustainable source of nourishment. This skill is essential for long-term survival in environments with limited food resources. Javier knew the guava fruit in the jungle was safe to eat, but someone with less knowledge than him may have selected a fruit that was detrimental to their health.

7. Learn Basic First Aid: Basic first aid skills are invaluable in survival situations. Knowing how to treat common injuries with limited resources can make a significant difference. From addressing wounds to managing basic medical needs, people equipped with first aid knowledge increase their resilience and ability to overcome medical emergencies in the wilderness. Jeremy in the desert knew how to treat his snakebite and Henry in the tundra knew how to reduce his bleeding and keep his wound clean.

HOPEFULLY YOU NOR I will ever end up in a harrowing survival situation like these folks did. But if we ever do, we would do well to remember each of these true-to-life characters and the skills they used to survive. The wild is unpredictable and sometimes unforgiving, but it can also provide us with the materials we need to make it out so that we can return to our loved ones. Ultimately, the knowledge of essential wilderness survival skills coupled with the will to survive is what we need to survive and thrive.

Astonishing Survival Stories from Around the World

To gain additional inspiration and survival knowledge, many readers have found my book *Astonishing Survival Stories from Around the World: Incredible Accounts that Inspire Indomitable Spirit* to be an excellent companion to this book. It is an engaging compilation of true and gripping survival narratives of people with uncommon resilience.

Presenting nine remarkable stories of individuals who faced extreme survival situations, the book highlights the harsh realities of nature and the importance of survival skills.

Recounting shipwrecks, plane crashes, and ordeals in the jungle, each historical account demonstrates the determination and resilience of the human spirit.

Through these narratives, the author aims to inspire readers and impart valuable lessons on survival, emphasizing the power of hope and the need for respect and preparation for the wild.

These are The Greatest Survival Stories Ever Lived!

Dive into this edge-of-your-seat world of survival where resourcefulness and resilience overcome the impossible.

• Could you survive without supplies in a small boat adrift on the Pacific Ocean for 14 months?

• How would you find your way through a Peruvian jungle after falling two miles from the sky—without a parachute?

Be inspired by **9 harrowing ordeals of astonishing survivors** who defied extreme odds with bravery, stamina, and resilience:

• **James Riley's ingenious methods of helping his crew survive** being shipwrecked, enslaved, and forced to walk the Sahara.

• **Ernest Shackleton's incredible leadership in Antarctica** that turned his shipwrecked crew's icy despair into hope fulfilled.

• **Louis Zamperini's survival of a B-24 plane crash in the Pacific** and Japanese POW camps.

• **Joe Simpson's nearly impossible escape from the frozen jaws of death in the Peruvian Andes**.

• The heroic & ingenious rescuers of **13 boys of a Thai soccer team trapped deep inside a flooded cavern** for 18 days. And more.

To feel the rush of adrenaline while learning crucial survival techniques, immerse yourself in these vivid accounts of extraordinary determination and indomitable spirit.

Phoenix MacLeod books

In closing, if extraordinary challenges ever alter your own hunting excursions - as were the outings of our characters herein, may you richly possess and aptly apply the practical skills to demonstrate extraordinary perseverance and one day share with others your very own *Amazing Hunting Survival Stories*.

Joyfully,
Phoenix MacLeod
Survival Wisdom from an Off-Grid Survivor
https://www.phoenixmacleod.com/

P.S. While each of us who are hunters wishes to return from our hunts unscathed *physically*, what brings real comfort and abiding peace *spiritually* is knowing that the LORD promises eternal refuge and security for the souls of those who seek Him and his righteousness.

Psalm 91 - My Refuge and My Fortress

He who dwells in the shelter of the Most High will abide in the shadow of the Almighty.
I will say to the LORD, "My refuge and my fortress, my God, in whom I trust."
For he will deliver you from the snare of the fowler and from the deadly pestilence.
He will cover you with his pinions, and under his wings you will find

refuge; his faithfulness is a shield and buckler.
You will not fear the terror of the night, nor the arrow that flies by day,
nor the pestilence that stalks in darkness, nor the destruction that wastes at noonday.
A thousand may fall at your side, ten thousand at your right hand, but it will not come near you.
You will only look with your eyes and see the recompense of the wicked.
Because you have made the LORD your dwelling place—the Most High, who is my refuge—
no evil shall be allowed to befall you, no plague come near your tent.
For he will command his angels concerning you to guard you in all your ways.
On their hands they will bear you up, lest you strike your foot against a stone.
You will tread on the lion and the adder; the young lion and the serpent you will trample underfoot.
"Because he holds fast to me in love, I will deliver him; I will protect him, because he knows my name.
When he calls to me, I will answer him; I will be with him in trouble; I will rescue him and honor him.
With long life I will satisfy him and show him my salvation."

Now THAT, dear reader, is the most excellent survival story of them all!

For those who love God and have been called according to his purpose, they shall dwell in him, our Protector, the safest dwelling of all, wherein:

For now, today: No evil shall overcome you. No temptation or test will overwhelm you.

And then, on that Day: There will be no more tears, crying or mourning. There will be no more pain, disease, or death.

The greatest danger to you in this world is anything that would keep you from eternity with your Creator.

Do not fear any who can kill the body but cannot kill the soul. Rather fear Him who can destroy both soul and body in hell.

The thief comes only to steal, kill, and destroy. Jesus came that you may have life and have it to the full – in him now and forever.

So please choose wisely this day whom you shall serve. As for me and my house, we will serve the LORD.

Please Help Other Readers

Do you know why the Dead Sea is 'dead'? It cannot sustain life because it only receives (water) and does not give back. So, it remains salty, stale, and stagnant.

We've each been blessed to be a blessing to others. Now is your chance to make a positive difference in the lives of families you've never met.

If you have gained knowledge and inspiration from this book, then be blessed by informing others of its benefits. Kindly **invest one minute to share your review.**

Please share a review

https://reviewprojects.phoenixmacleod.com/hunting

P.S. Thank you for your thoughtful action. Other readers and I genuinely appreciate your input.

Free PDF Booklet for You

Here's a FREE GIFT for your family!

To bring even more value to you, you are welcome to receive this **free PDF of a 50-page booklet with 120 fun and creative outdoor activities** (organized by season).

To **receive your free PDF** and very few emails informing you of my next book of survival prepping projects or incredible survival stories, visit here:

https://www.phoenixmacleod.com/familypdf

Printed in Great Britain
by Amazon

57370079R00073